True North

by

Kelly Collins

Acknowledgments

As always my thanks go to my husband and my children who make my life a pretty place to live.

To my sisters who are always there to lend a helping hand or a swift kick in the pants depending on what is needed at the time.

To my mother who is my biggest fan. Thanks for scanning my books for hours searching for that one error that needed to be corrected. Your eye is appreciated.

To my friends who read my books and love me anyway.

Praise and Awards

Chapter One

Sweat drips from my forehead. I swipe at my wet hair trying to get it off my face. Without the humidity in the air, your lungs want to shrivel and die with each breath, add in the heat and you have a recipe for disaster.

Disaster, that's exactly what I'm facing. Sitting outside of my broken down car on a lonely stretch of highway between Los Angeles and freedom was not my plan. I paid a mere nine hundred dollars for an old Toyota Camry, but I had hoped it would get me more than a few hundred miles outside of L.A. I knew I was in trouble when the oil light came on. I was screwed the minute the check engine light blinked rapidly, and the engine began to sputter. I pushed the green beast as far as it would go and pulled over to the side of the road as it died a slow death. I managed to choke out another mile before it coughed and collapsed, leaving me sitting here on the open highway with the sun high in the sky.

Sweat drips from my chin and lands on my chest. A

constant bead of perspiration pools between my breasts. With the car door open, I sit on the torn leather-like upholstery of the driver's seat, trying to protect myself from the sun. I don't know what's worse: the heat, or the feeling of despair.

Only two cars have passed in the same amount of hours. One cruised by while I was peeing behind my car, and one floated by without giving me a second glance. Who does that? Who leaves a woman alone on a deserted highway in 120-degree heat?

I sip on the Gatorade I purchased seventy miles ago. The last town I passed was very small; a gas station was all that it had. I filled up my tank, bought a drink and a Twinkie, and headed north.

Holding my head in my hands, I reflect on the last few weeks. His voice still echoes in my ears.

You fucking bitch, you know that you will never get away with it. How could you ever think you could outsmart me? I am the master planner, not you, not your father. I found you, and I seduced you with promises and sweet words of affection. You were fucking pathetic. Your father was worse. He was so intent on getting a son—any son, that he basically gave me a partnership to marry you.

I shake my head trying to forget it all. That was my

past; I have no plans for the future. I'm free now, free of
Tyler, free of my treacherous family, and finally free of
pain. My immediate plan is to get a ride to the nearest
town, get my heap of junk towed, and find a place with air
conditioning.

The heat rising from the asphalt gives the road a
wavy, wet look. I glance in both directions. Although, I
would rather head north, I am willing to go in any direction
if it takes me away from here.

In the distance, I see the sun reflecting off something.
I have no idea what it is. The last hour, I've been like a
nomad in the desert, seeing mirages of every type. I stand
and stare, hoping beyond hope the reflection morphs into a
vehicle of some sort. I'm ready to throw myself into the
center of the road to stop anyone.

I watch the glimmer of light in the distance and feel a
sense of relief when the distinctive outline of a vehicle
becomes clear. I begin to wave my arms wildly, hoping that
whoever is driving will see me and stop. The heat is
unbearable, and I'm beginning to feel sick to my stomach. I
won't last out here much longer. I'm sweating more than
I'm drinking, it won't be long before I'm past the point of
dehydration.

As the vehicle gets closer, I realize by the grill that it

is a truck. I jump up and down trying to grab the driver's attention. The truck whizzes by. I fall to the ground in a heap and cry. With my head hidden in my hands, I shed the tears that have been building up for the last year. I sob uncontrollably. My hope fades as fast as a pair of jeans soaked in bleach. I'm in such a state that I don't hear the truck approach, or the man driving it walk over to me.

A tap on my shoulder sends me scurrying backward in a spider crawl. My eyes shoot up to a large imposing figure looming in front of me. His shadow gives me much needed respite from the sun, but his presence alarms me. Fear squeezes my chest, forcing my pounding heart to pump harder. Where did he come from?

"Hey, are you okay? I saw you as I passed, but I didn't react fast enough to stop. I came back."

In a stupor, I stare up at the man. I have no words. My only reaction is to bury my head in my hands and cry. The stranger kneels beside me and talks softly.

"How long have you been out in this heat? Let's grab your stuff and get you in my air-conditioned truck. I can take you to the edge of town; there's a motel there, it's a dump, but it's clean. I own the bar across the street. We have cold drinks and hot food."

I feel his hand wrap around my upper arm and pull

me into a standing position. I'm dwarfed by his size. He towers over me in the most terrifying way, and yet I'm relieved that someone has finally stopped to lend a hand. I take my free hand and wipe the snot from my dripping nose. I must look a mess.

"Grab your stuff, we can get Todd to tow your car tomorrow."

I still haven't uttered a word; I reach into the car to pick up my purse, and take the keys out of the ignition. It strikes me as funny when I lock up my vehicle. It's not like someone can hotwire it and drive away. I'm pretty sure the engine has seized up. I have a feeling that this car is on its way to an early burial. I walk to the trunk and open it to retrieve my suitcase. I don't have much, just the essentials. I left my life behind, and that meant everything I owned stayed there as well. What I do have was purchased at a second-hand store. What I couldn't find there, I purchased at Walmart. I swing my bag from the trunk and walk to his truck. He sees me struggling to get my bag into the back of the truck and comes over to help me.

"Here, let me get that. You have to be spent. How long have you been out here?" This is the second time that he's asked me that question. I suppose I owe him an answer. I look at my watch to see the time.

"I've been stranded for nearly three hours. No one would stop." I almost begin to cry again. I catch the sob that is forming in my throat and swallow it down. I'm not sure if I'm swallowing my pride or my sorrow, but either way I could sure use a chaser right now. He puts his hand behind my back and ushers me toward the cab. I feel the air rush out as he opens the door. The frigid air is heavenly. I clamber into the cab and push my face toward the vent. I sit there until he enters the driver's side.

"Thanks for stopping."

"No problem. Let's get you into town. Don't you have a phone?"

Feeling better, I lean back into the seat and relax. I turn to my left to get a better look at my rescuer. He's a large man, tall and muscular, with biceps that stretch the cotton of his T-shirt to its limit. His hair is sandy-blond, and his eyes are almost slate blue, maybe gunmetal-grey. If he didn't have such a gruff look on his face, I would say that he has a kind face. His look is a stark contrast to his demeanor. He seemed pleasant as he was kneeling next to me, but now his questions are coming at me as more of an accusation than an actual inquiry.

"I asked why you didn't call someone? There is cell service in the area," he says gruffly.

I stare at him and notice his frown. I'm wondering if stopping for me has put a glitch in his day.

"No, I don't have a cell phone. My service was canceled, and I didn't want to set up a new service until I got to where I'm going." Saying that out loud makes me realize how poorly I planned this trip. There was no planning at all. I grabbed my stuff and ran.

"Where are you going?" He glances toward me and then back at the road.

"I'm not sure at this point, I'm just going. I'll know when I get there." It's the most honest answer I can give. I walked out of the courthouse this morning and over to the used-car lot. I handed over nine, crisp, one hundred dollar bills, and an hour later I drove off the lot and onto Interstate 5. I wound my way around and turned when I felt like turning. I decided to head north, and that's how I ended up on this patch of highway.

"Are you running from something? Who jumps in the car in the middle of summer with no destination in mind and no phone? Are you out of your mind?" The rough timber of his voice makes me feel like a small child being scolded by an angry parent.

I stare at him with my mouth agape. This man doesn't know me. How dare he make assumptions about me. I don't answer him. I look forward and gaze into the distance.

"How far until the next town? What is it called?" I see nothing in the distance and feel grateful that I'm sitting in his cold, comfortable truck.

"We have about ten miles to go. It would have been a very long walk for you – seventy miles back or twenty miles forward. The town is called Sugar Glen, but don't let the name fool you, it's anything but sweet."

Silence fills the truck's cab for the rest of the trip. I sneak a glance at my rescuer and realize we haven't even exchanged names. I suppose if he were interested in knowing mine, he would have asked.

I relax for the next few minutes and make up names for him in my mind. If he were a god, I would call him Thor. If he were a superhero, I would say Captain America with his boyish face and manly body. In reality, I bet his name is something simple like Jack, or Tom.

Up in the distance I see another mirage, or maybe it's the town. I'm not sure at this point. We arrive at the edge of town and true to his word, the first thing we reach is a shabby motel with a bar across the street. The sign above the bar says Last Resort. The motel is called Shady Lane. I would say that is an accurate description for a place on the outskirts of town.

He pulls his truck into the dirt parking lot of the motel and exits. I dread opening the door, knowing that I'm going to get smacked in the face with sweltering heat as soon as I leave the truck. I brace myself and push forward, my body slides from the cab, and my feet hit the dusty dirt lane with a thud. He pulls my bag from the truck bed and sets it on the ground in front of me.

"I'll send Todd over to get your car, he is the most reasonably priced in town when it comes to towing services. Do you have enough money to get a room for the night?" His behavior is confusing. He totters between hostile and civil. One moment he's gruff and the next he's nurturing.

"Of course, I have enough money, how much can it be? It's not the Hilton for God's sake." My nerves are on edge from the heat. I reach down and pick up my bag. "I'm sorry, I should have thanked you. Instead, I was rude. Thank you for picking me up."

"Okay, well, gook luck." He turns on his heel and walks around his truck. He climbs in and puts the vehicle in gear. Spinning tires stir up a cloud of dust as he drives away. I was certain he would drive directly across the street to his bar, but he didn't, he headed deeper into town."

Well, he must hate his grandma, or she's dead. The sleazy dealer should have had a sleazy name like Vinnie, at least that would put people on guard. Nope, his name was Ben. It's an innocuous name. I would feel safe around guys named Ben.

I stumble into the heat, rush across the street and into Last Resort. I walk into the bar and grill and notice I may be the only female in the place. Adjusting to the dark room after entering from the bright light of day, I find an empty table in the corner. I climb up onto a stool, take a seat, and look around at my surroundings. I would say this is probably what I would have described if you asked me to tell you what my idea of a biker bar looked like. I could have a field day in here making up names for people all day. I can already see the names flash in front of me. Names like Weasel, Frog, and Moose come to mind. The big guy in the corner probably goes by Tiny or Little Al.

Neon signs advertising every type of beer imaginable hang from the walls. The wooden bar seats twelve. Mounted above it is a classic Harley Davidson painted black with shiny chrome accents. The well-worn booths are placed around the perimeter and bar tables with stools are littered throughout the space. Off to the right is a small stage that looks ready for either Karaoke or live music.

Directly in front of the stage is a small empty section of worn flooring that would be perfect for three or four couples to dance.

It's nicer inside than the outside would lead you to believe. I look around at the people occupying the seats. I see mostly middle-aged men with beer bellies and beards. Biker bandanas are tied around nearly half of the balding heads. A younger crowd is seated to my left. Tougher looking men with tattoos and women who look rode hard and put away wet are playing darts and pool. It's difficult to discern some of the men from the women. All in all, they seem harmless and engrossed in each other.

I lean against the wall and wait for someone to come and take my order. After ten minutes or so I walk to the bar to see if I can get some service. I lean against the wood counter and wait.

"Ring the bell," says the man to my right. "He's probably upstairs." I pick up the bell at the end of the bar and shake it back and forth. Every eye in the room looks toward the sound. I blush under their stares. I hear the thunder of boots coming down the wooden stairs directly in front of me. I watch as the boots turn into a full-grown man.

"Hi, I was waiting for service, but it never appeared.

looking, young blonde walks in. She can't be more than eighteen. She makes a direct line to the bar and looks up at the man standing next to me. She's all doe-eyed and smiles as she beams at him. He says nothing but nods toward the stairs. She obediently walks up them. She reminds me of a Hannah and so in my mind that's what I'll call her.

"I'll be back in a bit." He trots up after the young miss "Hannah".

I stare after them. What the hell is going on here? He's short-handed, but seems to find the time for a quickie upstairs with a girl who probably just learned to tie her own shoes.

I hear the clicking of a glass on the counter and look in that direction. Standing at the end of the bar is my first customer.

"What can I get you?" I ask as I nervously wipe the counter in front of me. The man sits his beer mug down and tells me to fill it up with Bud. He then orders ten hot wings with blue cheese instead of ranch. I pour his beer and look around to find an order pad. I write the entire order out long hand and ask the man his name. He tells me people call him "Bug". That's one I wouldn't have guessed.

I search around for a window to pass my order thru. The only access to the kitchen is through the swinging door to the right of the bar. A grey-haired cook stands in front of the grill looking at me as I enter his domain.

"Bathrooms are at the other end of the bar, darlin'." He winks and points to the door.

"I'm temporary help. My name is Alexa Cross, and I have a food order. He looks at the scrap of paper I hand him and begins to laugh. "What? It says exactly what I need."

"Darlin', I need you to be less wordy. In an hour, you will be writing one of these every two or three minutes, and I don't want you to get carpal tunnel your first day on the job." He pulls me to the prep counter and writes CW 10 BC. "Something like this will do. If I have questions, I'll ask. Welcome aboard, my name's Bud, just like the beer, only I am fuller bodied and get better with age." He chuckles as he opens the freezer to pull out a bag of wings. "Listen for the cowbell. It means you have an order up."

I walk out the door and into chaos. In the few minutes I was gone, nearly every table has filled up. I reach for the order pad and make my way around the room. I have mentally numbered the tables so that I know what will go where. I begin to pour beer after beer and make my deliveries. In the distance, I hear the sound of a bell and rush to the kitchen to pick up my wings and drop off three

17

more food orders. Bud looks at the tickets and smiles.

"You're a quick learner. Audrey was a dumbass, and even after six months, she was still tryin' to figure it out. You should consider stayin'." He slaps my orders up on the board in front of him and begins to cook.

"Did you get my order of a burger and fries? I will collapse if I don't eat something soon."

"Nope, but I'll whip yours up right away. We can't have you sprawled out on the floor, the clientele might just use you as a carpet."

The next hour breezes past me. My pockets are chock full of dollar bills. I now see why so many people turn to waiting tables. You get cash every day, and your checks are just a bonus. Most servers don't make minimum wage though, they typically get a substandard hourly rate that when added to their tips makes for something just above the poverty level. I wonder if Mr. Bar Owner always pays minimum wage, or if he is paying me more because he shanghaied me into helping him out tonight.

I hear the clomp of heavy shoes on the stairs, and my eyes go directly to the place where little miss prom queen "Hannah", and the nameless man disappeared. As he descends the steps, I see him buttoning up his shirt. Of course he is, he doesn't even have the courtesy to fully dress himself upstairs. I bet he left her naked and wanting while he got what he wanted—what he needed. *You can't punish all men because Tyler was an ass,* my inner voice reminds me.

"How are things going?" He adjusts his belt as he takes his place behind the bar.

I narrow my eyes at him. I have no idea how things are going. I've done the best I can. I inhale deeply, catching a whiff of him as he passes by me. He smells fresh and clean, like soap and leather. I inhale his scent and let it cleanse my senses.

"I've broken two glasses and dropped one order of wings, but I'm getting the hang of it. I need to eat or I won't be able to continue. Bud made me a burger that's getting cold in the back. Can you watch things out here for a minute while I swallow it whole?"

"Yes, and take your time. I'm sorry I forgot to put your order in." He looks genuinely unhappy with himself.

"No problem, I can see that your mind was elsewhere." I look toward the stairs before I dash into the kitchen.

Nearly seven hours later, he locks up the front doors as the last patron departs. I wipe the tables and sweep the floor before I walk up front to leave.

"I'm out of here, you'll have to re-lock the door behind me," I call out to him.

"Wait up. I'll walk you across the street. You don't want to exit a bar alone this late at night." He shuts the cash register drawer he was counting and walks me outside. He pulls three twenties out of his pocket and puts them in my palm. His hand is warm, almost hot. I feel him shift his palm and place it on the small of my back as he ushers me across the street.

"Thanks," I say. I suppose I can use this to pay for my car to be towed. I meant to put towing on my insurance, but it slipped my mind.

"Listen, today was a crazy day for me. I had a lot of things going on, and I wasn't the most pleasant of people. I apologize. I don't think I even asked your name. I'm Zane."

"I'm Alexa. It's nice to meet you, Zane. Thanks for the ride, a meal and the job." I offer my hand for him to shake. He looks at my hand and then back at me. He doesn't offer me his hand in return. What a strange guy. Who names their kid Zane? I'm not doing well in the name game these days. I would have never come up with that one.

"Since you are going to be here for a few days, why don't you fill in at the bar? I could use the help, and you can probably use the money. It doesn't look like Audrey is coming back, so I have an open position. If I recall, you are going wherever the wind blows you, so it's not like you have any commitments. Why don't you let the wind settle here for a few days?" He gives me a questioning look. I almost see a bit of pleading in his eyes. Oh, those blue-grey eyes. I can see why the little blonde got all doe-eyed in his presence. He's the perfect mix of boy-next-door and bad-boy with a dash of mystery thrown in.

"Why don't you use the other girl that came in tonight? She appears to be happy to help you out in whatever way she can."

"I need her for other things. Besides, she's not old enough to serve liquor. Just give me a few days. I can really use the help."

I bet he needs her for other things I think to myself, as I remember the young blonde who walked upstairs and never returned. Curiosity gets the better of me and I find myself saying yes before I can think things through.

"All right, what time do I need to be there tomorrow

mirror behind the bar. My fair skin is pink from catching too much sun yesterday. My brown hair is pulled back in a ponytail. I dipped my hair in soapy water too many times last night while I was washing bar glasses to not pull it back tonight. I'm wearing a pair of comfortable jeans and a tank top. I push up the girls a bit hoping I can pull in more tips. I raked in over a hundred bucks last night. Imagine what I could earn if I looked halfway decent.

"Hey, boss man, do we have a live band tonight? I thought they were good last night. Who would have thought that three old geezers could put out a sound like that?"

"They're a favorite here at the bar. They're back tonight and every first weekend of each month. This crowd likes classic rock." He wipes down the bar a few times, but I notice that he keeps looking at me.

"What? Do I have something on my face?" I lift up on my tiptoes to see myself in the mirror. Everything looks normal to me with the exception of my red nose and cheeks.

"You look fine. You should wear sunscreen. If you keep letting the sun kiss your face like that, you'll be old looking before you know it. Your skin is pretty; you should take care of it."

I'm not sure if I should focus on the "you're getting old part" or the "your skin is pretty" part, so I opt to ignore both. The front door creaks open and a bouncy redhead pops in. She makes a beeline for the bar and begins to apologize immediately.

"I'm sorry I'm late. I finished up late with my other client." She looks up at him with a worried expression.

"All right, head upstairs and get ready, I'll be there in a minute."

She bounces up the stairs without a second glance our way. Is he really going to leave me again for another romp with a teenage girl? She at least looks like she might be old enough to have grown pubic hair.

Before he leaves to follow "Red" upstairs, I see another girl emerge from the staircase. She resembles the girl from last night, but I can't be sure it's her. Zane opens the cash drawer and pulls out two twenties. She giggles and pockets the money. Someone has to talk to these girls about self-worth. First of all, to sell yourself for forty dollars is preposterous, but to do so knowing that another girl is on your heels is crazy. What is wrong with this man?

Before I can say anything, he disappears up the stairs. The sound of the cowbell means dinner is ready.

By the time Zane comes down the steps again, he's

dating potential, but I wouldn't go as far as saying that I'm robbing them of a future. They are learning a skill, one that they can use throughout their life. I keep them on a regular schedule, which means they can count on the money. That's a benefit for girls their age."

"Girls their age? What the hell is wrong with you? I don't understand you. One minute you're the nicest guy and the next you're—"

"I'm what, an equal opportunity employer? A flexible boss?" he asks in a bristly manor.

"Argh…you're just you." I have no idea what I'm saying and I have no idea what he is. I only know that I'll be glad to leave in a week. I'll be keeping my eye on him while I'm here though. Even if that means I have to wait tables and pour beer.

Standing in front of my door, he waits for me to unlock it and walk inside. Before I can close the door, he pulls something out of his back pocket. He places a small box in my hand.

"Make sure you charge it. I don't want you to be without a phone. It's just a pay as you go model, but I loaded three hundred minutes on it to get you started. It will at least be something until you get to where you're going."

I stand in my doorway with my mouth open. He

reaches in and pulls the door shut. I peel back the drape and watch as he disappears into the night. Who is that man?

I pull my laptop out of my suitcase and set it on the table. I connect to the Internet and hear the pings of multiple emails arriving. I take a beer from my mini refrigerator and take a seat. Todd was nice enough to pick me up today and take me to see my car. My nine hundred dollar steal-of-a-deal car is turning into a twenty-four-hundred-dollar money pit. On the way back, he pulled through Walmart so I could get a few things for the week. I am normally a wine kind of girl, but with the severe heat, beer was a must have. I pop the top off and take a drink of the bubbly liquid.

I sit down and look at my computer screen. I used to love getting emails. It would mean that I'm either going to connect with someone I know, or I'm getting hired to do a job. Now that I decided to leave my past behind, the ping of an email sends my blood pressure skyward. I really should change my email address. I suppose on some level I'm not ready to say goodbye forever.

My inbox contains six messages; one is from my sister Ava. She says she misses me and wants me to call her when I get settled. One is from my mother who only says to call her. One is from my dad. I delete it before I read a single word. One is junk; it's an advertisement for that little blue pill that seems so popular these days. I would need an emergency room if my man had an erection for four hours. The commercial says if you experience that; seek medical advice. No shit. The fifth message is from him. I know I shouldn't open it, but I can't help it. I click open and see vile words spew across the page. My heart skips a beat, then races to catch up.

Dear,

That's a funny greeting...dear. It reminds me of you that morning when I took everything away—a deer in the headlights. You thought we had it made. I was running your daddy's company, and you were dabbling in your cute little computer craft. In the end, I got rid of you, got away with murder, and got half of your family assets.

Cheers,

Tyler

I'm gutted by this email. I tried so hard to bring charges against him. I was battling him and my father at the same time. He was threatening me, and my dad was more concerned with losing his business than losing me. In the end, he lost both. Tyler ended up the victor because, in our legal system, you can't be tried twice. It just goes to prove justice isn't always served.

By the time it was said and done, I had walked away with nothing but myself. What he took from me can never be replaced, but in the end I still have me. My only hope is to move forward. Physically, I have healed, but mentally, I don't know if I will ever be okay.

I scroll through the last message and see that Lone Star Development has hired me to do some independent contracting for them. I put in a bid before I left L.A. They need some code written for a project and I'm the girl to do it. I shoot off an email and tell them that I will begin the work on Monday. The money is good and the flexibility is important at this point in my life. I can work from anywhere. I figure if I get three or four jobs a year, I can live a good life.

I type a quick message to my sister telling her I'm fine. I have no idea what my long-term plans are, but I finally feel I can breathe. I struggle with the message to my mom; she wasn't the most supportive person when I was going through my crisis. She was more worried about whether her and my dad would land on their feet. I write that I'm doing well and will contact her in the future.

I take my beer and walk into the bathroom. This body isn't used to manual labor and being on my feet for over eight hours a day is killing me. I turn the hot water on high in the tub and pour the tiny bottle of shampoo under the stream; it's the only thing I have on hand to create bubbles. The heat from the water rises and fogs the mirror. I turn on the cold tap and blend it in with the hot, before I strip off my clothes and slip one leg at a time into the bathtub.

The heated water soothes my tired feet and legs. My manicure is a mess and my hands are beginning to crack from two days of washing them all the time. I have never been so tired, but I have also never felt so content. I have loved every minute of getting to know the townspeople. In a big city like Los Angeles, you don't get the opportunity to get to know people well. Everyone is so busy trying to make a life; they never actually live their life.

I've watched the desire for money destroy people. It was all Tyler wanted. He had a goal and he went after it. In the process, he destroyed many lives; he nearly destroyed mine, too.

I sip my beer and think about Zane. The man is an enigma. He is generous with his money, but he seems short on time. He obviously has little respect for women because he pays for their services, and yet I think that maybe it's better that way for him. He is a surly, bossy man. What kind of mate could he be? He's got to be swamped running his business. I believe it would be tough to have a relationship when you have such a crazy job.

His clientele seems rough at first glance, but after two days of working, I see they are just normal people trying to live authentic lives. I like my hair long, and so do many of the men that frequent Last Resort. I wear jeans and so do they, although many accessorize with leather chaps. I pierce my ears, and so do many of the people I serve. I bet they pierce many things. They have body art and I—well, I am thinking about it. I've noticed a few tattoos on the women I've met that are really pretty. Some were willing to share the stories of their art with me. One woman nearly lost her life from a ruptured gallbladder; the emergency surgery left a massive scar. She pulled up her shirt to show me a beautiful tattoo of a phoenix rising from the ashes. The wings hide her scar; her tattoo has meaning. She relates to the bird.

I toss back the remainder of my beer and climb out of the lukewarm water. I dry my body, apply lotion, don my pajamas and climb into bed. Just before I fall asleep, I remember I need to plug in the phone Zane gave me. I need to let him know I'm not destitute. I make good money, and I can buy a phone.

I must come across as down on my luck in my second-hand jeans and old used car. I just want to step out of my comfort zone and living thriftily is part of my plan.

I climb out of bed and open the box. Inside are the phone, the charging cable, and a note.

Alexa,

To keep you safe,

Zane

How sweet is that? He intrigues me and unsettles me at the same time. My experience with men is limited to my ex-husband, my father, and the few dates I had before college. High school boys were harmless. My father is a huge disappointment of a man and Tyler…well he…he's the devil. So, I don't know what to make of Zane. He's generous but callous. So confusing.

Chapter Three

I wake to a soft rapping against my door. My achy feet take a minute to adjust as I shift my weight and stand. I sleepily walk to the door. Trudy stands outside next to her stocked housekeeping cart.

"Mornin', Alexa. Do you want your room cleaned today?" I look back into my room as if it's going to answer for me. The king-sized bed sits with only half of it mussed up. If I want clean sheets, I can sleep on the other half.

"No, all I need are some fresh towels? If I can get those, then I think I'm good."

"All right then," she says as she reaches into her cart and pulls out two bath towels, a hand towel, and a washcloth. "Do you need shampoo?"

"Yeah, I'll take a bottle, it makes good bubble bath. How are you, Trudy?" I ask as she reaches into her plastic bucket to retrieve the shampoo I requested.

"I'm good, sweets. I wake up every mornin' and that's a good start to the day. I hear you're working over at the Resort. How is Zane treatin' you?"

"He's been good to me. I'm just helping out until Todd finishes repairing my car, and then I'm out of here."

"Well, it's been nice having you here. It's not such a bad place to be. You should think about stayin' on for a bit. I hear that you're a mighty fine waitress. That's gotta be a bonus for Zane after what he put up with from the last girl. That man's just too nice. Most people would fire a person if they showed up late repeatedly, but not him. He's just too nice."

"Well, Zane is an interesting man. I can't say that we've had much time to talk. He always seems to be running around like his hair is on fire. He pays me a fair wage, and he feeds me, so I would say he has been good to me." I wouldn't call him particularly nice, but I have no reason to believe differently.

"He's one of the finest men I know, and I know a lot of men. Most aren't worth rubbing two nickels together for, but Zane…he's a good one."

"I should go shower and eat my bagel. I have to be at the bar at noon. Don't work too hard, Trudy. Have a nice day."

"Same to you darlin'." I close the door but hear the creak of the housekeeping cart's wheels as she makes her way down the walkway.

I ponder her comments about Zane being a good man for a minute. I obviously use a different scale to measure upstanding behavior. In a small town, maybe pouring drinks down people's throats and banging their daughters in exchange for a few twenties is acceptable. Hell, when I think about it, my dad wasn't much different. He pretty much sold me to the highest bidder, who happened to be Tyler.

Tyler did his homework. I have to give him credit for that. He knew what company he wanted to work for. Why wouldn't he want to work for my dad's company, Alliance Space Technologies (AST)? It traded publicly, was worth millions, and my dad had no sons. Tyler found his in.

I remember our first date. He was the grader for my Calc II class. He handed me back my paper one day, and next to my "A" was a note that said, "Meet me for dinner." At the bottom of my paper were his number and the word, "please."

How can you turn that down? He was cute and charming, and we seemed to hit it off right away. He insisted on meeting my parents by our third date. From that point on, he became a permanent part of our family. My mom planned the wedding before he even proposed. I got sucked in. I didn't notice the signs, in fact, there weren't many. He was really good at manipulation, an incredibly smart sociopath. Over a period of four years, he wheedled his way into my heart and family. He got my dad to make him a stock holding partner and then everything changed. He treated me differently. I was no longer treasured or made to feel as if I had value. I didn't feel like the intelligent, self-assured woman I'd grown up to feel. In fact, I felt as if my own value had decreased as time went on and my self-worth depended solely on him.

Looking at the clock, I realize I have spent way too much time dwelling on the past. It's eleven-fifteen, and I still need a shower.

I slink into the front door with only five minutes to go until my shift starts. Zane is behind the bar, loading a fresh cash drawer into the register.

"Good morning, Alexa. How did you sleep?" He smiles broadly at me. I don't think I have ever seen him smile. He has perfectly straight, sparkling white teeth.

"I slept well, thanks. What about you?"

He laughs a bit and shakes his head as if he's entertaining some private joke. "I haven't slept through the night in months." He picks up his coffee and takes a sip. That's all I've ever seen him drink. He pounds back cup after cup every day.

"Maybe you should cut back on the caffeine. You would be able to sleep better if you didn't consume gallons of the stuff."

He looks at me thoughtfully. I see the corner of his mouth twitch, and I think that maybe he's going to grace me with another smile, but instead he just shakes his head and says, "If only it were that easy."

"It is easy, just switch to caffeine free or drink something else. Hell, you own a bar; have a glass of wine to relax. I find that one drink before I go to bed helps me sleep like a baby."

"Have you seen many babies sleep lately?" He smiles at me. I frown at him. The subject of babies is a sore one for me.

At twelve o'clock, our first customer walks in. He pulls off his leather vest and slaps it on the table. I walk over and get his order.

"What can I get you?" I ask.

"I'll have a Bud, and the old lady will have a whiskey and soda. Is Bud in the back cookin'?"

"Yep, I believe he is. Did you want something to

eat?" I inquire. I stand there holding my pad of paper waiting on him to decide. He's an older man with two earrings in one ear and a big American flag tattooed on his bicep. I tap my toe with impatience before he finally tells me, "Tell Bud, Hank wants his regular, chili cheese fries, with extra onion."

"I'll let him know." I turn to the bar and call out my drink order to Zane. I walk through to the kitchen and slap my order on the counter for Bud.

"Tell Hank hello, would ya', Lexi?" He smiles at me. It's as if he likes getting under my skin.

"It's Alexa and I'd be happy to pass along your greeting." I leave the kitchen to pick up my drink order.

"Thanks," I tell Zane as I pick up the drinks and walk them to the table. Hank's wife has arrived. She's an average-looking normal person. She isn't wearing leather, has no tats, and has a single piercing in each ear. She reminds of my kindergarten teacher, Mrs. Klause.

"Here you go," I say as I place the drinks in front of my first two customers of the day. "Bud says hello."

I turn around and head back to the bar. Zane is staring at me.

"What? You're always staring at me. What's wrong now? Did I age fifteen years since yesterday because of my sunburn? I couldn't help getting burned. I was stranded in hell for nearly three hours. When you get that hot, you're going to get burned."

"Are you always this grumpy, or just with me? Watch the counter," he demands as he walks up the stairs two at a time. I wonder what's up there, an office, storeroom, maybe a love shack?

My thoughts are deferred by the arrival of a large group. They file through the door and take seats around three of the pub tables. *Perfect, he leaves and I get swamped.*

I plaster a fake smile on my face and trot on over to take their order.

"Hi, what can I get you today?" I look around the group and play the name game to take my mind off Zane's last comment. Was I grumpy? He's the grumpy one, always barking out orders. I don't need this shit. I thought working here would occupy my time and my mind until I get to where I'm going.

"Did you get all that?" the grizzled old man standing in front of me asks. He reminds me of Grizzly Adams, so I mentally call him Adam.

"Uh, no, I'm sorry, I was distracted." I smile at the bearded man and give him my full attention. How embarrassing, my mind was so preoccupied I didn't hear anything he said.

"I think it came out to two Buds, three Bud lights, two shots of Jack and three wheat beers with lemon slices. We would also like fifty hot wings and an order of fries and rings."

"All right, I got it. By the way, what's your name?" I wait to hear his answer.

"It's Abrahm. What's yours?"

"I'm Alexa, and it's my pleasure to meet you. I'll have your order up in a few minutes." As I walk away, I give myself a mental high five. At least I got the first letter to his name right. I had a one in twenty-six chance. The odds were not in my favor.

Just as I'm pouring the last beer I see Zane appear from the mysterious room upstairs.

"What else do you need?" He places his hands on my hips as he passes behind me. His large hands almost circle my waist as he moves me aside. I kind of like the feel of his hands on me. Maybe those girls are getting the better end of the deal. They get paid *and* get his hands on them. "Alexa, where are you?"

"You don't want to know." I gather my drinks on one tray and heft it up to my shoulder. I maneuver through the bar and sit the heavy tray successfully on the table in front of my customers.

"Your food should be out in a few minutes. Can I get you anything else?"

"Nope, we are all set. Bring us another round in fifteen minutes."

"Will do." I pick up my tray and head back to the bar.

"It shouldn't be as busy today. Sunday is all about the little rushes. We have a lot of biker groups stopping by, so they come in clusters, but intermittently."

"All right." I reach around him to pick up a wet soapy rag out of the bucket. I want to wipe down the tables. I inhale the scent of him as my face passes his shirt. He always smells like he's just showered. It's soap, leather and something almost sweet. I've smelled it before, but I can't put my finger on it. "Do you always smell this good?"

"I don't know if I smell good, but I showered a little while ago. I'm glad I don't stink," he replies with a chuckle buried in his response

Blushing at my lack of tact, I work around him. He takes the cloth from my hand and tells me to relax.

"You're a hard worker. Are you sure you haven't waited tables before? You act like you have done it all your life." In the background, the Juke Box plays AC/DC "Back in Black".

"Nope, this is a first for me. I've entertained at my house, so I know how to make people relax and feel comfy, but I've never been a waitress." I look at him and can almost see the wheels turn in his head. His expression is thoughtful and questioning. His right eye is twitching a bit.

"What's your story?" He walks around the bar and sits at one of the empty stools. Just as I begin to answer him, the cowbell rings.

"That bell is for me," I say. "Can you pour me another round?"

I walk toward the kitchen and he heads for the taps. By the time I come out with the wings, onion rings, fries and condiments, he has already delivered the drinks.

"I'm not sharing my tip with you," I tease.

"That's all right, I make a decent living on my own. So tell me, what's your story?"

He is persistent if nothing else. Each time I can't or don't answer the question, he just asks again.

"I don't have a story. What do you mean? I'm just a girl who is figuring some things out."

"I get that, but who is this girl that has a fifty-dollar manicure and wears Walmart jeans? I've been trying to figure you out for a few days." He leans on the bar with his chin on his steepled fingers.

"Well, contrary to your initial perception, I'm not down on my luck. I have a job. I'm a computer programmer. I do contract work. I also owe you for a phone." I cock my head and smile.

"Why did you say yes to working here then?"

"Like I had a choice. You told me I owed you. You tossed an apron at me and disappeared." I raise my eyes and scrunch my mouth.

A robust laugh escapes his mouth. I can see it comes from deep inside his core because his whole body is shaking with laughter.

"Do you always do what people tell you? You could have told me to kiss your butt."

"That's not really my style. Anyway, I did owe you, and you looked like you could really use the help. Since I'm stuck in town for a bit, I thought it would be a good distraction." I look around the bar and wonder how he got here. "What made you become a bar owner? You don't look like your customers."

"I'm exactly like them. There is nothing that I would rather do than pull my Harley out of the garage and take a road trip. Unfortunately, my life has taken some turns lately that prohibit me from doing that."

"I'm sorry to hear that. I'll be right back." I walk to my tables and make sure that everyone is taken care of before I return to our conversation. I find Zane deep in thought.

"What are you running from?" he blurts out when I return. "You have a new car, well not exactly new, but it has temporary plates. You have no phone, and you have no place to go. What has you running? Are you in danger?"

I ponder his question for a moment. I suppose I'm running, but not from anything specific, I'm running to something, something that I haven't named yet.

"I'm not in danger. I'm not running as such, I am exploring my options. I left a bad situation, and I'm making my life better. I do have a phone…now. Thank you." I lean against the counter crossing my arms over my chest. "Are you from here? Have you always lived here? We're all running to or from something, aren't we?"

Another laugh but this one is more of a "you have to be joking" kind of laugh.

"I moved here two years ago and purchased the bar. My mother settled here after her retirement and then became ill. I came to help. If I'm dashing out of the bar, it's usually because she needs me for something."

"That's really sweet. I'm sure she appreciates that.

What did you do before owning the bar?" I watch him as he formulates his answer. His face has scruff on it; he must not have shaved today. It takes his baby face away and gives him a gruffer look— one that matches his everyday personality.

"Believe it or not, I lived in Los Angeles and worked as a financial analyst for an investment firm. I spent my weekends on my bike. I loved to ride down the coast. The salty ocean air blowing in your face is fabulous."

"You're not too far, you could still head to the ocean on the weekends. I'm sure you can get someone to watch the bar so you could go on occasion."

"I've got too many commitments these days." He looks off into the distance as if he's reliving a memory. "Have you ever been on a bike?"

"No, I have never ridden on a motorcycle. They are dangerous. I don't even like to ride a bicycle."

The door opens and our next rush walks in. Two couples take seats in a corner booth. I scurry over to take their drink order. The man raises his hand in a wave to Zane. "Hey man, how are you? How's the family?" he calls out.

Zane walks over from the bar and pats the man on the back. "Things are good. I can't complain."

"Glad to hear it. We're taking a ride in two weeks to Calabasas. You should join us. We're leaving Friday night and coming back Monday around noon. Think about it."

"I will."

I leave them to finish their conversation. I didn't mean to hover, it's just that I haven't seen him interact with his customers, and watching his eyes light up at the mention of a weekend ride makes me smile.

I pour the drinks and set them down in front of the foursome. I pull a stool over for Zane so he can sit and visit with his friends. I pat him on the shoulder and tell him I'll hold down the fort while he talks. The smile he gives me warms my heart. I suppose there is a softer side to him after all.

Customers float in throughout the day. It's never really insanely busy, just bursts of business. In between, I managed to wipe the entire place down.

"Why are you doing that?" he asks.

I turn to him and answer. "It needs to be done. Since you're paying me, I'm not going to sit on my butt and do nothing. It's not in my character to just wait for the next thirsty person to come in. I have to keep busy."

"I don't think the bar has been this clean since I bought it. Are you sure you can't stay? You're the best thing that's come through that door in a long time."

His statement paralyzes me for a moment. It's been years since anyone has paid me a compliment. I think the last time someone said something remotely nice to me was when I cut my hair and Tyler said it didn't look that bad.

"Thanks. I appreciate that." In the background, Aerosmith's "Sweet Emotion" fills the air. I grab my dishrag and dance around the mostly empty bar wiping everything in sight. I look toward the bar and see Zane's eyes watching me. His lips are turned upward into a smile.

I lock the door after the last customer leaves and queue up Queen's "Bohemian Rhapsody". I feel happy and carefree. I haven't felt this good in years. I belong to me and no one gets to control me anymore. I dance around feeling the rush of freedom. For the first time since I left Los Angeles, I feel like things are going to be all right.

Zane closes out the register while I sweep and mop the floor. Just as I'm beginning to have pleasant thoughts about him, a chubby brunette descends the stairs. She waits at the register for her pay. She exits without a glance in my direction. I never saw her enter today, but he did disappear upstairs several times throughout my shift. He always came back down looking happy and relaxed.

I put everything away and walk out the door. I don't

wait for him to walk me across the street. I don't want to be around him right now. I understand that men need sex. I understand that he's busy and can't commit to a relationship, but it gives me the creeps knowing he's upstairs screwing somebody while I'm serving up beer and wings below. This is his business and he should be down here taking care of it. Why is it that the men that I meet, always want to take something from me? With Zane, it's my time and energy. I've given enough.

"Hey, wait up. I can walk you," he calls out from the door.

"No worries, I'm good," I yell back as I reach the other side of the street.

I slip my key in the door and escape his madness once again. My car should be ready by Friday. I'll pack up everything Thursday night and be on my way Friday morning.

I grab a beer from my little refrigerator and open my laptop. I hold my breath as it starts up. The ping of incoming emails makes my breath hitch. What will it be today, another stab to my heart? A reminder of what was stolen from me?

I scour the emails and see none from the devil and release the breath I was holding. My sister emailed with a message of love. After I read the four other emails, I close it up for the night.

Just as I am getting ready to hit the sack, I hear an unfamiliar chiming coming from the nightstand. I go in search of the annoying beep and realize the phone Zane gave me is ringing. I don't recognize the number and figure it's just someone calling by accident. I ignore the call and go about my nightly ritual. Less than a minute later I hear the sound again.

"Hello?" I answer the phone with a question in my voice.

"Thank goodness. I thought maybe you didn't charge the phone."

"Zane, is that you?"

"Yes, I need a favor. I need you. I've called all of my regulars and none of them can come right away. Can you come here, now? It won't take long. I'm desperate."

I can hear the panic in his voice, but the message he's delivering doesn't compute in my brain. "What the hell? She was just there."

"I know it's terribly inconvenient. I know it's late, and you're tired from working all day, but I'll make it worth your while. You can rest here. My bed is really comfortable. It's a life and death situation, or I wouldn't ask. I'll meet you at the door of the bar." He hangs up abruptly.

I stand in my room dumbfounded. Did I say I would go? Of course not, but he did sound desperate. Can a man sound panicky from lack of sex? His young little thing just left thirty minutes ago. Why would he need me? I mean we talked today, and I got to know him a bit, but not enough to want to give it up to him.

I throw a hoodie over my pajamas and slip on my tennis shoes. I'm going to have to set this man straight. I'll walk over, tell him to kiss off, and let him know I won't be working Tuesday. I have my project to start tomorrow anyway.

Chapter Four

I grab my key and march across the street ready to give him a piece of my mind. I stood by for years while my ex-husband made me into a shell of myself. I'm not about to let another man use me, take what he wants, and then toss me aside.

By the time I get to the door, I'm furious. He opens it and before I can say one word he takes my arm and rushes me upstairs.

"This is my house. Everything you'll need is on the counter. My cell number is on the phone I gave you. If you forgot it, the landline is here." He points to a table next to the sofa. "All of my numbers are on the refrigerator. I shouldn't be more than a couple of hours. He just went down to sleep so he shouldn't wake up for a while. His food is in the refrigerator." I watch as he frantically races around the room, grabs his keys and his jacket, and dashes out the door.

"What? What the hell are you talking about?" I call after him. He doesn't respond, just jumps in his truck and takes off like he's being chased by demons.

I'm left speechless and alone in the middle of the room. I turn around in a circle, taking in my surroundings. So this is the upstairs. I never considered it could be a house. I thought maybe an office or storeroom, but his home never crossed my mind.

I walk around the room taking it all in. It's a big open space. I slowly rotate in a circle and process everything I see. To my right is the kitchen; it's sleek and modern with white cabinets and stainless steel appliances. To the right of that is a dining table. It is round and made of dark wood. Six beige, upholstered chairs surround it. In the center is a bowl that seems to be a catchall. I can see coins, bills, and a half-eaten roll of Tums. Next to the Tums is a pacifier. I rotate further and see the door where Zane exited. When I open it to get a better view, I see it leads down to the back yard. In the center of the lawn sits a swing set and a teeter-totter.

I close the door and walk farther into the living room. A massive television takes up an entire wall. *Leave it to a man to decorate.* Across from the wall are a brown leather sofa and two chairs. The coffee table that sits in front of the sofa is littered with newspapers and books. I begin to straighten things up when I see the book that brings it all together for me, *From Birth to Toddler.*

You have got to be kidding me? I think, and then it all comes back to me. The young girls and his constant disappearing act. He was always freshly showered and he smelled of something sweet. That scent was baby lotion or powder. His gruffness is probably caused from lack of sleep. My eyes dart to the pacifier on the table. Why didn't that raise a flag? I just skimmed over it.

My heart begins to beat wildly in my chest. This can't be happening to me. I can't take care of a kid, even for a minute. I'm not equipped to handle it. I have no idea what to do. I pace back and forth in the room. I glance up and see a hallway and know I will eventually have to venture down it.

I feel myself start to hyperventilate and know I have to get my breathing under control. If I don't, Zane will find me passed out on the floor, and his kid will be left unattended. I sit on the sofa and put my head between my legs. I repeat the mantra my therapist gave me. I begin *So-Ham, Ham-Sa, So-Ham, Ham-Sa*... breath in on the So-Ham and out on the Ham-Sa. It's an effective tool to get myself under control. The loose translation in Sanskrit is "He I am" and "I am he", which in my way of translating means, "I got this shit."

When I finally feel comfortable enough to pull away from my knees, I look at my surroundings more carefully. The signs of parenthood are everywhere. In the corner is one of those plastic frames that has crazy stuff like animals and rings hanging from it. A basket full of pacifiers and teething rings sits smack dab in the center of the coffee table. The corners of the square table has pads attached to it. A stack of diapers and a box of wipes sit at the end of the sofa.

How could I not see that? *You saw what you wanted to see.* I hear my inner voice and she's right. I've seen what I wanted to see since I arrived. I didn't see a dedicated father. I saw a sex-crazed man. I didn't see a kind Samaritan, I saw a man who bristled and grumbled and told me I owed him.

I'm ashamed of myself. How did I become such a cynical person? I was never that girl. I used to see the good in people. I was the embodiment of a Pollyanna. If you looked up Pollyanna in Webster's Dictionary it would have said, "a person characterized by irrepressible optimism and a tendency to find good in everything" and after that it would have said "Alexa".

I let him change me; I let them all change me. Between my mother, father, and Tyler, they sucked the joy and optimism out of my life. If I continue to be like this, it means they win. I need to find myself and get back to the Alexa I once was - the girl who laughed so much she snorted. I want soda to spurt out my nose. I want to sing when I shower. I want to dance in the rain and have water balloon fights in the heat of the day. I want to live again, not just exist

I square my shoulders and tiptoe down the hallway. I open the first door and find a king-sized bed, neatly made. Two nightstands and dresser complete the room. There are two doors in this room. One door leads into a large walk-in closet. I enter and inhale. It smells exactly like he does. He smells fresh and clean, with a hint of leather and baby powder. It's a weird combination, but somehow works for the man who flips between gruff and gracious on a dime. I run my fingers along his clothes and bring a shirtsleeve to my nose and inhale.

I walk in a circle around his closet and see that he has mostly jeans and cotton T's, and some button-down shirts. In the corner is a leather vest. I pull it out and see his name stitched onto the right breast. Turning it around I see the back that has a patch of an adult hand and a child's hand locked together. The initials BFK are stitched above the clasped hands. I have no idea what that means.

I venture into the next room thinking that his child might be in there but only find the most fabulous bathroom. In the corner sits a large Jacuzzi tub and next to it is a separate shower with a bench. The double-sink vanity is directly across the way. Being the nosy girl I am, I open his medicine chest and see only staples. Things like aspirin and Band-Aids. I feel guilty looking through his personal stuff, but that doesn't stop me from opening a few drawers. I find the majority of them are empty; only one contains anything, and that is a razor, brush, and comb.

I leave his personal space behind and venture down the hallway. The door to my right is open, and I can tell right away it's a bathroom. It smells heavily of baby shampoo. I flip on the light and see a tub full of toys. The tub's tap is covered with a rubber elephant snout. In the corner is one of those shampoo rings shaped like a duck. The idea is to put it on a kid's head. When you shampoo and rinse, the water rolls off the sides and never gets in the baby's eyes or ears. *I wonder if it works?*

I open the next door to my left, and find an office. At least I was right about one thing. On the wall hangs his diploma. He finished his degree three years before I graduated from USC. That would make him roughly twenty-nine or thirty years old.

There is one door left to open. This one is slightly ajar. In the distance, I can see the movement of light. I creep into the room, trying to make as little noise as possible. On the dresser is the source of light I noticed before entering. It's rotating and throwing images of stars and moons onto the wall and ceiling.

I slip farther into the room and come up next to the crib that is dead center on the wall. In the dim light, I can barely make out the theme of the bedding, but I think it's the cow jumped over the moon. What is that nursery rhyme? I think goes something like— hey diddle, diddle. What the hell is a diddle?

I peek into the crib and see a sleeping infant. I listen to his even breathing and hear his lips root around for something to suckle. Since my split with Tyler, I have avoided anything to do with children, marriage or couples. Looking at this infant, I am consumed by emotion. I want to reach out and stroke his hair. I gently touch his downy soft locks, trying not to wake him. His hair is dark in this light. His skin feels like velvet; it's so soft and supple. I gently rub my hand down his back and stop to feel him breathe in and out. I brush one finger along his arm and trace down until I reach his tiny little hand. He startles, and his arms and legs flex out. When he relaxes, his little palm closes tightly around my finger.

I look at this little human grasping my finger. Tears begin to spill from my eyes. This very moment will be imbedded in my mind forever. This baby, whatever his name is, has marked my heart in a way I can't explain. The rocking chair is just a few feet from my grasp. I can't grab it. I refuse to release his hold on me. With my toes, I take hold of the leg and slowly drag the chair toward me. I settle in next to this little man and wait for his father to return.

In the silence, I have nothing to distract my thoughts. I begin to question how a man like Zane ended up with an infant. By the looks of this baby, and I'm no expert, he can't be more than a few months old. Where is this child's mother?

While I was snooping, I didn't come across anything that would indicate the presence of a woman. His closet was full of men's clothes; his bathroom didn't have makeup, curling irons, hair dryers or tampons.

I thought the man was an enigma before, now he's just a puzzle that I *have* to figure out. What man takes care of an infant by himself? There is a story here and I have every intention of figuring what Zane's story is all about. All the things that irritated me before, I now find endearing. Reality changes everything. When I thought he was trotting upstairs for a quickie with a teen, I was disturbed and disappointed. I should have called him on it, but something about his demeanor didn't match his actions. I think I knew deep down inside he wasn't up to anything bad.

Now I know he's taking care of an infant, running a business, and trying to take care of an ailing parent, I have a whole new level of respect for him. I lean my head against the rungs of the crib and watch his little boy sleep. In a matter of moments, I begin to doze.

Did you think I would allow that? I don't want that. You were careless and inconsiderate. You didn't even think about what I might want. Haven't you figured it out? This is and will always be the Tyler show. There's no room for Alexa, and there certainly isn't room for that shit.

I startle awake and realize it was just a dream. Actually, it happened, but my mind is obviously working it out through my dreams. I look through the bars of the crib and see the baby begin to stir. What will I do if he wakes? I bolt from my chair and rush into the living room to get the book. How do I warm up formula? What kind does he have? There are different types, right? He said something about his food being in the refrigerator. I am ill equipped for this job.

I walk into the kitchen and open the refrigerator door.

The top shelf contains a can of formula concentrate. I read the directions to find out I need to warm up two ounces of water for every ounce of formula. How much does he eat? I look around and see a case of bottled water. I locate a pan and measure eight ounces of water into it. I'm going to be prepared if he wakes up. I put the water on low to get in just above room temperature.

I walk back to the living room and begin to read the book. I cover the section on holding a baby, diapering a baby and feeding a baby. I put a cover over my warm water and turn the burner off. Feeling a bit more prepared, I make my way back to his bedroom and take my seat in the rocker.

I got what I needed. I got exactly what I was after. It took four fucking years of my life, but I'm set forever. Do you know how awful Wednesday nights were for me? It was hump night. I had to take you at least once a week, so you didn't think anything was wrong in our marriage. I loved it when you were indisposed with your monthly cycle, because then I didn't need to touch you. I don't even like women. You thought Friday nights were poker nights. I looked forward to Friday, it was the only day I could be myself. It was the only day I could be with him.

I wake to the soft whimper of a child. I quickly take

in my surroundings and realize I am at Zane's watching his son. I look at my watch and see it's been four hours since I arrived. Whatever made him shoot out of here like a bullet from a gun must be serious.

I walk to the kitchen to prepare his bottle. When I am satisfied that I won't burn his little tongue off, I sneak back into the room. I approach the bed and see the little guy looking like a skydiver. His arms, legs and head are all off the bed. He teeters on his belly until his neck muscles can't hold him up any longer. He plants his face into the mattress and begins this exercise again. I watch a few rounds before I hear the frustration in his voice. He calls out to me with one shrill scream. It's not a cry; it's more of a warning that things are going to escalate if someone doesn't intervene. I set the bottle down and reach in to pick him up.

With my hands under his armpits, I pull him to me. I wonder if he notices I'm a stranger? If he does, he doesn't let on. He simply pushes his face into my breasts and begins to root around. I'm not sure if this is a baby thing or a man thing. I had a suspicion that men's obsession with boobs started at birth, and this just confirms my belief.

I cradle him in one arm and sit down in the rocker. He is getting impatient with my inexperience. You can tell that he's used to getting what he wants right away. I grab for the warmed formula just as his scream pierces the night. With one swift move, I line up the nipple and silence him.

Snug in my arms, he suckles on his bottle. I watch his cheeks draw the milk in. A little dribble escapes from the side. I pull my finger across his cheek catching the drip. I mindlessly wipe it on my pajama bottoms.

I read that a baby should be burped intermittently and so to his dismay, I pull the bottle from his mouth and shift him over my shoulder. I see a thick receiving blanket hung over the crib. I put that over my shoulder and place him on top of it. With gentle taps, I urge the air to escape his stomach. After a few pats, a big burp emerges. Who would have thought that could come out of a baby as small as he is?

Happy with our progress, I continue the feeding. This time his need to feed is less urgent. I look into his eyes and see happiness there. There is a twinkle that shines from him. He gums the nipple and looks as if he is smiling around it. I pull the bottle away from him and listen to him coo. "Hey, little man, what's your name?" I ask. I know it's silly because he can't answer, but I just feel the need to talk to him, to let him know I'm here and will take care of him. I will protect him while he is mine. I whisper to him about lots of things. I tell him my hopes and dreams, and I tell him that he has a great daddy. I watch as his eyes begin to droop. I know I should put him back in his crib, but I can't bear the thought of letting him go. He feels so good in my arms.

I feel his weight shift and sit up abruptly feeling as if I might drop him. When I open my eyes, he's gone. Zane is standing above me looking exhausted. His baby is sleeping peacefully in the crib.

"Hey, I'm so sorry." He helps me up from the chair and guides me out of the room. He closes the door slightly and walks me down the hallway. "I can't thank you enough."

"It's okay. It was a bit of a shock at first. I had no idea you had a child."

"Well, it's a fairly new experience for me as well." I watch him reach into his wallet and pull out a few twenties.

"No, I don't need the money, Zane. Let's just say that I'm a friend helping out a friend."

He looks at me and puts his money back in his wallet. "I owe you an explanation." He pulls me to the couch and forces me to sit.

"You don't owe me anything. However, I would love to know the name of your son. I called him little man all night. It would have been nice to say his name."

He pulls his hands through his hair and groans. "I'm so sorry, I was in a panic and none of the girls could come right away. I didn't want to take him to the hospital because there are so many germs there and he's so little. His name is Aaron Michael Abbamonte, he's three months old, and he's amazing."

I see his tired eyes light up, and a look of peaceful contentment washes over his face.

"Little Aaron is a doll. I fed him and rocked him."

"Did you change his diaper?" he asks as he moves his head from shoulder to shoulder as if trying to crack his neck.

"Oh my God, no. I'm an awful babysitter. I just wanted to comfort him, and so I fed him. He's probably lying in a pool of his own urine." Tears pierce my eyes and I begin to sob. I don't know what's come over me. "I tried to take care of him, but I failed him."

I feel the sofa shift as he scoots closer to me. His arms wraps around me as he pulls me to his chest. I breathe him in. What I smell calms my nerves, and I switch from all out blubbering to an occasional whimper.

"You didn't fail him. You met his immediate needs. Kids are quite forgiving, and I'm sure he won't hold it against you. He's been in a wet diaper before, and I guarantee he will be in a wet diaper again. Hell if he hates it that much he will learn to potty train early or change himself." He chuckles lightly. The movement of his chest rubs against my cheek. I flush at the intimacy of our position. I push off him and sit back.

"Alexa, I really appreciate you coming over on a second's notice. My mom had fallen at the home she lives in, and they thought she had broken her hip. I met the ambulance at the hospital. As it turns out, she just bruised it badly. I should get you home so you can get some rest."

"On no you don't, I slept while I was here. You need to grab a few good hours of sleep before the little man wakes up again. I read some of the book that is on the table. It would appear that babies his age have a ravenous appetite and no real need for continuous sleep. Go climb in bed, Zane. I will hold down the fort for a while. Off you go."

He gives me a wary look. I see him waver between going to bed and arguing with me. In the end, he stands up and heads toward his room.

I sneak down the hallway about fifteen minutes later and peek in on Zane. His breathing is deep and steady. I pull the door closed as I back away. I walk to Aaron's room and gaze at him for what seems a lifetime. His tiny hand is fisted up near his mouth. His tiny lips suck on his knuckles.

He doesn't seem to upset over his wet diaper.

I tiptoe out of his room and walk back to the living room. Curling up on the couch, I doze.

Did you really think I loved you? I wish it were that easy. Alexa, you're a likeable girl, it's just that I never did like you. I liked the package deal you came with. You took down walls that would have taken me years to breach. Honestly, it was your father's money and power that got me hard. That's what I was after. Unfortunately, I had to marry you to get it.

"Alexa, wake up. It's okay." I hear his voice and feel the soft stroke of a hand across my hair. I flail about, thinking it's Tyler. The thought of him touching me makes my skin crawl. "Alexa, shhhh it's okay. I heard you whimpering. It looks like you were having a bad dream."

I settle down and curl up on my side. I'm trying to wrap my brain around what's happening. His hand softly caresses my cheek. His fingers push my errant hair away from my face. His thumb runs under my eye, grabbing the tear that must have escaped. I relax under his care and inhale deeply. I've missed the touch of a man stroking my skin. It has been so long since anyone has touched me. I wish this moment could last forever.

In the background, I hear the beginning sounds of an

unhappy baby. Zane rises from the couch to take care of his son.

"Can I get him? I owe him a diaper change. I would also love to see what the little man looks like in the light of day."

"Sure, he's all yours. He seems to like the ladies. I would certainly rather wake up and see your beautiful face instead of mine."

I ignore his compliment and hurry down the hallway to redeem myself.

Chapter Five

I pick the little bundle up from his crib. In the morning light, I can see that his bedding is indeed a depiction of Hey Diddle, Diddle. On the cover are fiddle-playing cats and moon-jumping cows. His room is painted powder blue and contains everything a baby could want or need. I hold him out in front of me while his legs dangle and kick. I see that he is soaked through and it breaks my heart that I didn't change him on our previous date.

"We need to stop meeting like this, little man. Your daddy says that your name is Aaron. I think that's a fine name. You and your dad have it covered from A to Z. Let's get you out of those wet clothes." I pull him close and feel his wetness soak through my PJ's, but I don't care. He feels so good in my arms.

We walk to the dresser where I pick out his clothes for the day. On top is a tiny pair of blue shorts and a red, white, and blue striped shirt. I transfer him to the changing table and peel off his wet clothes. I pull back the tabs on his diaper and rid him of the ten-pound weight.

"Careful, there is something about cold air and its stimulating effect on his bladder." Just as he finishes his last word, a fountain of pee shoots directly for me. I try to stop the stream with my palms but only manage to create a bigger mess.

Zane rushes to help me. I bust out in laughter. I reach down and flick Aaron's nose. "Funny little man, aren't you?"

"I tried to warn you," Zane says. He looks at the pee drip from my chin and laughs. He pulls out a wipe and cleans me up with it. "I'm going to give him a quick bath and get him dressed. You should jump in the shower yourself."

Disappointed that I'm being dismissed I slump my shoulders and walk toward the door.

"There are towels in the cupboard and if you look in my third drawer down, there are some shorts with a tie at the waist. In my closet are my T-shirts. Grab whatever you want. I'll meet you in the kitchen when you're done." He picks up his naked son and follows me out the door. He turns off into the bathroom a few steps into the hallway as I continue to his room.

In the shower, I take hold of his bar of soap and bring it to my nose. It's a scent I recognize. It's his scent. I scrub the night's sweat and Aaron's pee from my body. I giggle at the thought of what happened. Little man gave me a golden shower and I was okay with it. His arms and legs kicked and wiggled like he was enjoying his ability to make a direct hit. I watched his little smile as he got a bulls-eye to my chin.

I let the water pour over my head and run down my back. Why do I keep reliving my nightmare in my dreams? I almost forgot the last one. The shock of waking up with Zane comforting me made me forget what had disturbed me in the first place.

I pour his shampoo into my hands and work it into a rich lather. I rinse and look around for conditioner. Of course, he doesn't have any, why would a man need a de-tangler or conditioner. Hell, the fact that he has shampoo is shocking. He could be the kind of man that thinks a bar of soap is multipurpose.

I step out of the shower onto the bathmat and reach into the cabinet for a towel. Even his laundry smells like him. Why am I so obsessed with his smell? I pull on the shorts and cinch them tight with the drawstring. I could put two of me into these shorts. I toss the black T-shirt over my head and let it fall. It reaches my knees. He must shop at the big and tall store. I could wrap a belt around this shirt, and wear it as a dress. Who needs the shorts?

I look in the mirror and frown. My face is flush from the hot water, and my hair is a mess. I reach into his drawer and pull out his brush and drag it through my hair. I put some of his toothpaste on my finger and "brush" my teeth. Feeling clean and refreshed I head into the living area.

As I reach the end of the hallway, I hear him talking to someone. Not wanting to disturb his conversation, I slink into the living room, trying not to make a sound. I lean against the wall and watch him. Aaron is lying over his left forearm. His little legs are hanging next to Zane's elbow, and his head is cradled in his hand. Zane is gently bouncing him up and down and speaking softly to him. I listen intently.

"Let's make some pancakes for our guest, buddy. We have to make up for your lack of etiquette. You're not supposed to pee on girls, they don't take too kindly to that. You're lucky that you're cute, and she has a good sense of humor."

I continue to watch the scene unfold in front of me. Aaron seems to answer his dad. His cooing and gurgles almost sound like a response to his dad's chiding. My heart clenches at the heartwarming scene. Here is this big man who is obviously in love with this little boy. I wish I had a picture of this moment to remind me that some fathers are good.

"What do you think she will like? Should we fix her our special blueberry pancakes, or just keep them plain? You were a lucky man last night to have her holding you against her breast. I walked in on the two of you and almost felt jealous."

His statement takes my breath away. He felt jealous of his baby? I didn't even think that he took notice of me. He always seems so grumpy and out of sorts. I suppose I should cut him some slack, he's got a lot going on. I keep my eye on the sweet pair in front of me.

Feeling like I am watching something that wasn't meant for my eyes. I decide to interrupt the intimate family moment between father and son. I clear my throat and walk toward the kitchen.

"Look at you, all full of surprises. I'm impressed that you can hold a baby, and cook at the same time. Let me help, either give me the little man or hand me the spatula. I have limited experience with both, so choose wisely."

He begins to laugh. The sound reverberates from his chest and makes its way out of his mouth in a melodic fashion. His laugh has the deep tone of one of the famous tenors. Looking from the spatula to the baby, you can tell he's debating.

"Although I would love to see you in the kitchen, Aaron would probably prefer to be in your embrace than slung over my arm."

I whoop with glee; I was hoping that I would get the baby. I would have happily flipped pancakes, but snuggling with this little, baby-powder fresh, bundle of joy, makes me giddy with happiness.

"Yes! I was hoping that I would get you. Now that your junk is covered I can rest easy." I lift him up by his underarms, and I gently swing him around. He gets a shocked look on his face and for a minute I'm afraid he is going to cry. I pull him down and into my arms where he roots against my breast. "Did you feed him? He seems to be looking for something to eat."

Zane looks at his son frantically moving his head back and forth against my breast.

"He's definitely my son. I suppose he's going to be a breast man He just ate so it's not about hunger. He just likes the boobies."

I pull him away from my chest and rock him back, cradling him in my arms. His arms flail around in an attempt to get control of his body. He's left a large drool mark on my borrowed T-shirt. I can certainly see why his daddy has to shower or change several times a day.

"Just like a man. However, I didn't know that your gender developed a predilection for women's parts so early in life."

"Oh, it just starts there, from that point we zoom in on everything. There isn't a part of a woman that I wouldn't worship for hours. I can tell he's going to be a ladies' man. He's already got you hooked and it's been less than a day."

"Is that why you keep him hidden upstairs? I had no idea your house was up here. I saw you heading upstairs with all of these little girls and well…"

"Well, what? What did you think I was doing up here with high school students?"

I lower my head and turn in shame. I had all sorts of awful thoughts about him and what he was doing.

"Oh hell, did you actually think I was…holy shit, Alexa. What kind of man do you think I am?" His tone has changed from playful to gruff. I know how to deal with gruff, it's mostly what I've seen since I arrived.

"What was I supposed to think? Pretty young things would show up and disappear upstairs, and you would emerge some time later buttoning your shirt or freshly showered. A short time later, the girl would come downstairs and you would hand her a few twenties. You called them your regulars. What was I supposed to think?"

He stands there and stares at me. In the moments that follow, I feel sick to my stomach. He says nothing until I point out that he's burning the pancakes.

"Shit!" He removes the pan from the stove and dumps the blackened pancakes in the trashcan. He sprays the pan with oil and pours more batter into it.

"I'm sorry. I know better now, and it all makes sense, but until last night I had no idea what you were doing or dealing with." I rub my lips along the baby's head and revel in his soft skin and baby fine hair.

"Tell me, when I called you last night what did you think I was asking you to do?"

My cheeks must have turned bright red because he begins to grumble. He slaps a few pancakes on two plates and comes to the table.

"Why did you come over if you thought I wanted to hire you for sex? I don't see you as that type of girl. Did I read you wrong as well?"

The last part of his question punches a hole in my chest. I read him wrong from the get-go, and I passed judgment on the kind of man he is—what I thought he was.

"No, I came over to set you straight, but you dragged

me upstairs, rattled off a slew of directions, and ran out." I pull at the single tear that falls from my eye. I have never been so ashamed of myself. I'm not the kind of woman who makes snap judgments. Tyler took so much away from me, and my ability to read people is one thing I need to get back. I can't move through life thinking all men are bad.

"I can understand how you could get the wrong impression. I didn't think to tell you that I had a baby upstairs. He's my number one priority right now, and I'm trying to make it all work. One day I was a bar owner and the next day I was a father. It literally happened that fast. I'm playing catch up. I have only recently felt like I had a handle on things and the last few days have been the best. You breezed into my life, and somehow things seem easier. You handle the bar as if you've been doing it for years. It's given me the time to straighten a few things out. Thank you."

I just accused this man of being a lecher and he's thanking me for helping him out. "I don't deserve your thanks. I passed judgment on you. I'm not normally like that. I've recently been through some of the toughest months of my life, and those events have changed me. I'm trying to find my way back to me. I've lost my compass."

"I understand. We're all finding our way."

We sit in silence and eat. He makes a killer pancake. I still have the baby cradled in my arm. He has fallen asleep. His little bowed lips flutter as he breathes in and out.

"Zane, can I ask you a question?" I look into his eyes trying to convey my sincerity.

"Sure, I think with you, I need to be an open book. Next, you might think I have bodies buried in the basement."

I gasp at the thought. "There's a basement?"

"No, what's your question?" His bristly grumpiness is peeking out.

"Where is Aaron's mom?"

He looks at me and then looks down at the baby in my arms. His expression softens each time he looks at Aaron. I can tell that he loves his little boy beyond everything else.

"I couldn't honestly tell you. We weren't a couple. We hooked up a few times when she was in town."

"Wow, you said earlier that you were a bar owner one day, and a daddy the next. You make it sound like you weren't prepared for his arrival. Surely, you had months to prepare."

The roar of his laughter startles Aaron. His arms fly

out. He pulls them back and falls into his peaceful slumber. I gently stroke the dark brown curls on his head.

"Sorry, I didn't mean to laugh at your question. I was laughing at the situation. I found out about Aaron the day he was born. I received a call at five in the morning from Tabitha, saying, "I just had your kid, you need to be here today, or he's going up for adoption." She gave me the hospital name and the city she was in and then hung up. I closed the bar for the day and headed to San Francisco. When I showed up, the nurses had my name written down at the desk. They brought me to the nursery and wheeled a baby in a plastic crib to me. The nametag on the crib said, "baby x." She didn't even give him a name. I was told that she gave birth and left. I fell in love with him the minute I saw him. I was a total goner when I held him. I paid their hospital bill and brought him home."

"You had no idea? A woman calls you and tells you she had your kid, and you came running? You're an amazing man."

"All I could think of was my son was not going to be adopted out, when I had the means to care for him. What man would give up his child?"

The tears well up in my eyes. I want to run—to escape, but I have this little bundle in my arms and I'm stuck.

"Hey, I have to get back to my home away from…" I stall on the last word because right now, Shady Lane is my home. "I have to go. Let me help clean up and I'll be on my way. Thanks for breakfast." I stand up and hand Aaron to his dad. I pick up the plates and move them into the kitchen.

"Leave them, I can do them in a bit. Why are you rushing off? You don't have to leave. I'm not asking you to go. I would rather you stay."

I rush around trying to tidy his kitchen. I need to go. I stop what I'm doing and tell him, "I can't stay. I have a job, and I need to work. I have a deadline to meet."

"That's right, you mentioned something about a job. Tell me about this job. What is it that you do to pay your bills, Alexa?"

I lean against the kitchen counter and speak. "I'm a contract worker and I write computer code. I prefer to be called a computer programmer, but I'm often called a software engineer."

His eyes grow large. A smile spreads across his face.

"I shanghai a genius to wait tables, pour beer, and then further demean her by asking her to babysit. I'm sorry, Alexa."

"Don't apologize. The last three days have been some of my best in recent months. I have loved helping out in the bar. I've met so many nice people. I had this preconceived notion about who bikers were and what they were about. I've been schooled. Most of them are just normal people living real lives. I play this game with names. I love to guess what people's names are, I'm almost always wrong, but the bar is a great place to practice."

"What was my name?" he asks. He looks at me intently. He always seems to have a scowl on his face.

"Does that scowl always work for you? Do you just intimidate people into giving you what you want?"

"It doesn't seem to work with you." He shakes his head.

"I called you Jack in my head, I considered Tom, but neither were correct. In the end, it was a victory because your name had four letters and so did Jack."

"You have a very flexible grading scale."

"Hey, you have to take your wins where you can get them." I look around the kitchen and decide it's as good as it's getting. I scoop up my dirty pajamas and head toward the door.

Zane's hand reaches up to the door making it impossible for me to open. "Come over for dinner tonight.

Aaron and I are going to BBQ. He makes a wicked good barbeque chicken." I look at the sleeping baby and the man holding him. I could lose my heart quickly with these two. I can't afford to open myself up for injury again.

"I can't, I'll be working all night. I'll see you tomorrow. What time does my shift start?"

He looks happy at the mention of my returning to work.

"How about four o'clock? The bar is open until midnight so if you want eight hours, then come at four."

"I'll see you then. If you can have a W-4 Form ready for me, I would appreciate it. As a money man, you have to know that paying me under the table is not good for your business. Weren't you like a bean counter or something like that?"

"Yes, something like that."

I lean down to kiss the baby on his head. I feel his daddy's lips brush against my head. My hair stands up on my arms, and a chill runs down my spine. I don't feel fear, I feel something I never thought I would feel again—desire. His free hand reaches around me as he opens the back door. I leave the only two men who have softened my heart in months. One is a shameless womanizer and the other is his father.

Chapter Six

I have been sitting in front of this laptop for three hours. The table is littered with empty wrappers from the box of Nutty Bars I devoured for lunch. Empty soda cans are lined up like targets at the state fair. Maybe ingesting the equivalent of a small child's weight in sugar wasn't the wisest choice.

Looking at my project, I imagine it will take me two to three weeks to straighten their shoddy code out. You would think that a company as big as Lone Star would have checked everything out before they published it. I've only been working for a few hours and I can see all sorts of errors.

This isn't my favorite type of work. I prefer to code for games because it doesn't seem like work. I get to write a bit and try it out. I've become quite the gamer. Coding tax software sucks. I imagine it's probably as boring as being an accountant or tax preparer.

I get up from my chair and stretch. Bending my body in half, I let my arms dangle to the floor. The blood rushes straight to my head, maybe that wasn't such a good idea. I right myself and hold onto the table for support as my head stops spinning.

I've decided to allot myself a break. With the remote control in my hand, I relax on the bed and channel surf. I find the *Game Show Network* and settle in for an hour of *Wheel of Fortune.* It's obviously much harder to play in person than when you are sitting in the comfort of your own living room, or in my case, a motel room.

I find myself yelling at the contestant named Mary, whom I would have bet money on that her name was Trish. She doesn't look like a Mary. It's too bad we can't call kids something temporary while they establish a personality. Who thinks to name their kid Stone, or Rapture? It's tough enough to be a kid, but to be a kid and saddled with a name like that, your parents had to be masochists or high when they named you. Thank God Zane named his boy Aaron. I looked up the meaning earlier and Google said it meant, "Warrior Lion". That's a big name for a little boy to fill.

Frank Zappa named his kids, Dweezil, Moon Unit, Diva and Ahmet. The only one that got a remotely decent name was Ahmet. Maybe he was named before Frank got uber rich and famous. What is it with rich people naming their kids? Names like Ivy Blue and Apple can only come from someone who thinks they are above public opinion. I hope these kids go to private school, or have bodyguards to fight the big fights.

"Can't you see that it's Social Butterfly Collection?" I scream at the TV. It's the easiest before and after I've ever seen. Mary turns the wheel and lands on $1000, all she needs to do is say "L," and she's racked up $4000 dollars. I hold my breath and wait for her to pick a letter, but the idiot buys a fucking vowel. Who does that? Mary asks for an "A." Of course, there is only one. Do you think she could've been smart enough to pick a vowel that would get her more than one tile turned? Mary chooses her next letter and *hallelujah* she calls out an "L." The tiles begin to turn, and I am perched on the end of the bed, waiting for her to solve it. When I hear her call out "Social Butterfly Collection," I hop off the bed and dance around the room.

God, I need to get a life. Is this what my life has become, overdosing on junk food and game shows? Maybe I should just cut my losses and buy the cat now.

I sit down at the office I have set up on the table and get back to work. I leave the TV on for background noise. It doesn't seem nearly as lonely when there is noise in the room.

Four hours later, my eyes burn and my stomach

begins to growl. Looking at the bedside clock, I realize I haven't eaten anything but the snacks from earlier. I begin to rummage through my stash of food. I have all kinds of microwaveable things to choose from. There is beef stew, chili, mac and cheese, and my all time favorite, Beanie Weenies.

Sadly, none of my options sounds nearly as appealing as BBQ chicken at Zane's. I should have said yes, but I feel out of my element right now. I have no idea how trustworthy my opinion is, and I'm not sure how I feel about Zane. Everything I thought he was, he isn't. I was wrong from the beginning.

I used to believe that I was a good judge of character. I trust people until they give me a reason not to, and honestly, I would give them one more chance even if they screwed me. I have to wonder why the bells and warning lights didn't go off with Tyler? How could I stay married to him for four years and not know that things were off?

We went through the motions of a happy marriage. I suppose I should have known—should have seen the signs. We didn't make love as often as we should have. Aren't newlyweds supposed to fuck like rabbits?

He worked late many nights and hung out with his male friends on the weekends. I was busy establishing myself in the field. Trying to make something with what Tyler referred to as my "Computer Craft".

I remember the exact moment I should have recognized something had changed. It was about three weeks after our wedding; I dressed sexily for him. I lay sprawled across the couch when he came in. He glanced at me, tossed his coat at me, and walked into our room. I waited a few minutes thinking that he was toying with me. When he didn't come back to the living room, I went in search of him. I found him sound asleep in the guest room.

The fact that he walked past me without lifting an eyebrow should have said something. What hot-blooded man can walk past a near naked girl and not respond in any way, except to humiliate her by throwing his jacket over her. It told me he didn't find me attractive. I spent the evening crying myself to sleep—alone. That's when he started to sleep in the guestroom. I should have said something then, but I made excuses for him. He was tired. He was stressed. He didn't feel well. He drank too much. *What an idiot I was.*

I'll admit that I'm not a ten, but I would give myself a solid seven to an iffy eight. I'm not fat, but I'm not skinny. I have meat in all the right places. I've never had men complain about my body, or my sexual prowess, so when my young husband only wanted sex on Wednesdays, that did something to my self-esteem, and I still haven't fully recovered.

Feeling the need to clear my head, I change out of Zane's clothes and into my own. I grab the room key and head out to take a walk. The sun is sitting lower in the sky and with that comes a cooler temperature. It could reach 120 degrees during the day and drop down to 40 at night. Tonight it's warm with a slight summer breeze.

I'm on my third lap around the parking lot when I notice the distinctive aroma of BBQ chicken. The scent draws me in like a magnet to metal.

"Hey," I call out as I round the corner of the building. "I can smell that chicken from across the street. I had to come over."

He swings around with barbeque tongs in his hand poised to attack. Recognition spreads across his face by way of a smile.

"You startled me. I wasn't expecting anyone to sneak up on me."

"Well, that's usually what happens when someone sneaks around to your backyard. I didn't mean to catch you off guard." I make my way toward him and peek around his body at his culinary fare.

"The offer is still open if you want to join me and my little buddy for dinner." He looks over toward the stroller by the table. I walk over and peek in at the sleeping baby.

"I was hoping you would say that. I looked at my microwave options and none of them enticed me." I look back at Zane and see that his mood seems light and carefree.

"Why don't you watch the chicken, and I will get the fixin's from upstairs. Do you want me to bring you a beer?"

"Are you having one? I don't want to drink if I'm drinking alone."

"I'll have one with you." He turns and takes the stairs two at a time. His well-defined calf muscles flex and relax as he runs up the steps. Dressed in cargo shorts, a T-shirt and boat shoes, he looks like a prep—not a biker.

I turn around and begin to flip the chicken. I hear his distinctive step coming down the stairs. It's like a cadence from a drum-line. I feel his presence directly behind me. The hiss of the bottle as he twists the cap off, whistles in my ear. His hand touches the small of my back making my body feel weak in the knees. I turn quickly and find my face planted in his chest. I sniff trying to get a whiff of him before he moves away, but he doesn't budge. He stays there with his chest in my face. I tilt my head back and look into his eyes. We stand in silence staring at each other. Breaking the silence, he steps back and holds out a bottle of beer for me.

"Thanks." I pull the bottle up to my mouth and take a long, slow drink, my eyes never leaving his. The intensity between us is palpable. It's like there is a fissure of electricity arcing between us.

His head dips down, and I would swear he was going to kiss me. In that minute, I wasn't sure if I should let him, or move to the side. The decision is made for me when he leans to the side, and grabs the tongs.

"I invited you, so you get to sit and relax. I'll cook. We are having baked beans and corn on the cob as well." He points to the table at the dishes he brought down. "Hand me those foil-wrapped corn, and I'll slap them on the grill. I coated them in butter, salt and pepper, and placed a few fresh basil leaves in the packet."

"That sounds yummy. So, I'm thinking, that you like to cook." I look at the chicken cooking to a perfect crispy golden brown. "How did you become a financial analyst?"

"I was always good at math and decided to use that, in conjunction with the business management degree, I earned. I went to a California college and made some connections through my biker club. When I graduated, I was already working as an analyst. I look at people's financial records, and I can spot their mistakes very much in the same way that you probably can when you're looking at HTML."

"Does it shout out to you? I look at code, and it's like the errors flash in front of my eyes saying *here I am*. I can just scan a document, and it becomes 3D in my eyes with the errors popping off the page."

"Yes, but in my case I see financial errors as red. They aren't red, but my brain sees the discrepancy and color codes it. It's always been easy for me. I was balancing my mother's checkbook when I was six."

"Wow, my checkbook hasn't been balanced in a year. I should bring it over to you."

"I would love to do that. Bring it to me."

"I just might do that." My stomach begins to grumble. "When is the chicken going to be finished? I'm starving. I've only had candy and sodas since breakfast this morning."

He frowns at me. "You need someone to take care of you. You should be nicer to your body."

"What? Now you're going to tell me that I will age fifteen years because I eat shitty food? I've had a lot going on in my life lately. I'll get back to taking better care of myself when I'm not living out of a motel room."

"No, you look fabulous. I think you're beautiful. I just worry about you because you don't eat well, you don't wear sunscreen, and I bet you don't exercise."

"Have you been looking at my cellulite-pebbled thighs? How do you know I don't exercise?" I brace my hands on my hips and give him my best *don't go there* look.

"You're a computer geek, you sit in a room all day in front of a screen. You probably pour soda down your throat and nap during your lunch break." He checks in on the baby, who is still sound asleep. "I only saw your legs today, in my much too baggy shorts, but from what I saw they looked amazing." His eyes twinkle with mischief as a slow smile lights up his face. "I'm happy to take a closer look if you need me to."

I blush from his flirty behavior. It's been a very long time since any man has complimented me. "All right. You're not too far off the mark, but I don't see you pumping iron or jogging three miles a day. So what gives you the right to judge my fitness routine?"

"You don't see me exercise because you don't get up early enough. Aaron and I jog five miles, three days a week. We start early, before it gets too hot. You should come with us tomorrow."

"You and Aaron jog…how?" My lips twist with skepticism.

"I have one of those three-wheeled jogging strollers. Aaron tends to sleep through the experience." Zane picks up a dish from the table and walks back to the barbeque. He piles the chicken and corn on the plate and walks to the picnic table.

I slide into the bench while he sits across from me.

"What do you like?" he asks, with his tongs ready to dish up whatever I want.

"I like the legs and thighs. What about you?" He plops a leg and thigh on my plate and picks up a breast for himself.

"Ah…a breast man. That seems to run in the family." I wink at him as he smiles.

"Yep, I love a succulent breast." He stares directly at my boobs. Thank God I changed out of his clothes earlier and back into mine. His clothes were like wearing a pup tent. It's not like what I'm wearing is sexy, but my jeans and tank top are better than what I was wearing earlier.

"Are you flirting with me?" I cock my head to the side and help myself to the baked beans and corn.

"Yes, I think I might be. Should I stop?" He takes a

bite out of his chicken; his eyes never leave my face. A bead of BBQ sauce runs down the corner of his mouth. I reach over and swipe it off with my finger. I pull my finger into my mouth and suck it off. An audible groan escapes his lips. My initial reaction is to laugh. I try to suppress my giggle, but end up bursting into a full on, belly aching laugh.

"Sorry...sorry, I'm not laughing at you, I'm just laughing. I don't think a man has groaned at me in years. I like it, and no I don't want you to stop." I look down at my plate trying to look at anything but his reaction. If there is anything other than a smile on his face, I'll be crushed. I slowly lift my eyes. When I reach his face, there isn't a smile; it's more like a shit-eating grin. The kind of smile a boy gets after he's copped his first feel.

We sit in companionable silence for a minute before he begins to talk again.

"Why don't you stay here for a while, at least stay until you finish your project? You don't have to hole up in your motel room; you can always come hang out with my boy and me. I could also use the help at the bar." He looks at me with pleading eyes.

I contemplate his suggestion for a minute. I don't have anywhere to go, and I would love to see more of

Aaron. He is the sweetest baby ever.

"Tell you what, I will stay for a few weeks on one condition." I contemplate how to address my stipulation. "I saw how your face lit up when you were talking about a weekend ride with your friend from the bar. I think you should consider going. I know you don't know me that well, but I would love to spend the weekend with Aaron if you would trust me to do that."

"Wow, I wasn't expecting that condition. I was thinking something like having to do your laundry, or feed you dinner every night. I didn't expect you to selflessly volunteer to watch my son so I could take a weekend ride."

"I know it's silly of me. I just thought that raising a child by yourself has to be exhausting. Who gives you a break?"

"I have babysitters. They're all very good. I paid for them to get training through the Red Cross."

"What the hell? What planet do you hail from? I know you're not from here." I raise my hands, palm up, and look around. "I have never met a man like you."

"I don't have much choice." He looks at the stroller and then back at me. "My mom would love to help, but she lives in assisted care because she has Parkinson's disease. She shakes so badly that she would never be able to hold him."

"I totally forgot to ask about your mom. How is she?"

"She's good, she's back at her home. She has a good bruise, but thank goodness she didn't break anything."

"Will I ever get to meet her? I would love to meet the woman who gave you the name Zane. Did you know it means God's gracious gift?"

"Actually, I did know, and that meaning is probably why I got the name. I'm the baby of the family. I have an older brother named Tyson, and a sister named Lisa. I was the last child she was going to have, so she decided that I was her gracious gift. As for meeting her, sure, she would like you."

"That would be awesome." I bounce a bit in my seat. "As you know, I love names, so I am always looking them up."

"What does Alexa mean?" He takes a bite of his corn and wipes the juice that runs down his chin.

"It's a derivative of Alexander and means 'to defend.'"

"Wow, I can see you being a protective person. I think you would defend someone you love to the death."

I feel a lump build in my throat. This discussion is getting way too personal for me. I look out over the yard.

My next question is an attempt to change the subject.

"Did your house come like this when you bought it?"

"What do you mean? Are you asking if there was a house over the bar?"

"No, I wanted to know if it looked like it does now, when you bought it. It's amazing. I love the kitchen, and that tub and shower are to die for. The décor is very man cave, but I like it, it's comfortable."

"When I bought the bar, it was in shambles. It had been abandoned for a few years. I got a great deal on it." His eyes gaze at the top floor. "I had the upstairs gutted and gave the downstairs a facelift. I made sure to have my house soundproofed to the extreme. You can't hear a sound when you're upstairs. Little did I know then, how important it would be now."

"How did you meet Aaron's mom? You don't have to answer, I am just curious." I put my last spoon of beans into my mouth and chew.

"She used to ride through town on occasion. We would casually hook up. I didn't even know her last name until I got his birth certificate."

"You know that the average man would have never done what you did."

"I don't know, I don't think you give men enough

credit."

"You could be right, I haven't had many responsible men in my life."

He looks at me and frowns. "Here's the thing. My father abandoned us when I was eight. He walked out one day and never came back. I remember sitting on my bed crying. I blamed myself for his leaving. That morning, I asked him for lunch money. He tossed me a dollar and told me that I was sucking the life out of him."

"Oh my God, that's awful." I reach forward and grab his hand. He opens his palm and folds it around my hand.

"The worst part was that I thought *if only I hadn't asked for a dollar. If I had just gone without lunch that day, maybe he would have stayed.*" He uses his thumb to stroke my hand. "I know better now. He didn't leave because of me, he left in spite of me, and that hurts more. He had kids, and he didn't give us a second thought. I promised myself then that if I ever had a child, they would become the center of my universe. I'm not willing to let my past hurt influence my future joy."

I could just kiss this man. He's an anomaly. I sit holding his hand and hope that he doesn't let go of mine. His touch brings me joy, something I've been without for a long time. I need this—need him. He sits here and holds my hand and has no idea how complete I feel in this moment.

"This morning you were having a bad dream. You were crying in your sleep. You kept saying 'how could you Tyler?' Who is Tyler?"

I sit for the longest time thinking of the best way to explain who Tyler is, without going into too much detail. I don't want to relive my past tonight.

"Tyler is my ex-husband. We were married for four years. We divorced last year."

"Oh…well…you waited a long time to run." He squints his eyes at me as if trying to solve a puzzle.

I look at him, stunned. He's a very perceptive man and doesn't miss much.

"There was a civil suit after our divorce. Let's just say that it didn't end in my favor. I walked out of court Friday and headed north—well actually northeast. The rest you know."

"I'm afraid I don't know much, but I hope that someday you will trust me enough to confide in me. I know what hurt looks like, and I see it in your eyes."

"Shall we clean up?" I look at him and notice his eyes look sad too. I suppose if I want him to trust me with his son, I should trust him with some of my secrets.

We gather the dishes, and the baby, and walk upstairs. I know I should head home, but Aaron is awake and I want to play with him. I steal him from his father's arms and rush him to his room so I can change him. This time I plan to guard myself against his geyser.

"You don't have to change him. I can do it. He may have a dirty diaper." He walks up behind me and cages me in. With one long arm on each side of me, I am trapped between him and the changing table. My heart is all a flutter.

"I want to do it. I hope to prove to you that I'm responsible enough to watch your son while you take a break." I remove the baby's shorts and T-shirt and get to work on the diaper. Thank goodness it was just a wet one. This is my first diaper change ever.

I dress him in a onesie and get ready to pick him up. His dad is still behind me. I can feel the heat of his body sear my back from his nearness.

"Wait," he says as I begin to pick up the baby. I stop and release him. What did I do wrong? I feel his hands on my shoulders. He turns me to face him, and I see something in his eyes. I turn back and pick Aaron up. I'm so afraid he will fall. Twisting back toward Zane, I see his focus is on my lips. "I'm going to kiss you," he says.

He bends over and lightly touches my lips with his. It's more of a drive-by than a head-on collision, but I like where he's taking me. He brushes my lips again. I feel his hand wind through my hair and pull me forward. He deepens the kiss. Our lips are fully engaged, but our tongues are absent from the mix.

I slide one hand up his chest and wrap my arm around his neck. As soon as I run my fingers through his hair, the kiss becomes very different. Before, he was kissing me, and I was enjoying what he gave, but I offered nothing in return. With my hand gripping his hair, I am a willing partner ready to match him.

Our tongues mingle together. I fold into his body wanting to stay in his embrace forever. I suck in the essence of him—his taste—his feel. I am safe with him. Everything about this feels right. He feels right.

Aaron makes a frustrated screech, which brings us both back to reality. I slowly remove my hand from his hair and drag it slowly down his chest before I back away. The last thing I do is remove my lips from his. It's as if I've been glued to him. Breaking the kiss is almost unbearable. I can't help but wonder if he feels the same?

I hug the baby to my chest and kiss his head. He smells like baby powder and barbeque. My eyes raise to look into Zane's. I see his warmth as he watches me hold his child, and I know deep in my heart that what we shared is way more than a kiss. Breaking the uncomfortable silence, I ask, "Do you want him, or can I hold him for a bit before I go home?" The thought of leaving twists at my heartstrings, but I know I can't sleep on his couch every night.

"You can hold him. I'm sure he would love that. It's time for his dinner. Can you feed him while I clean up?"

"I would love that." I carry him to the kitchen and prepare his bottle. Everything seems relaxed and normal in spite of the kiss we just shared. I watch as Zane tidies the kitchen and notice that there's easiness to his demeanor that wasn't there before, he seems comfortable—content.

I enter the living room and sit on the couch. I watch Aaron's little eyes smile as he sucks voraciously at the rubber nipple. Every few ounces I stop and burp him. He manages to suck the bottle dry at the same time as his dad finishes the dishes. *Perfect timing.*

"I should be going. I have more work to do. Thanks for feeding me." I hand the baby to his father, and reluctantly head to the back door.

"Are you going to go run with us tomorrow? We will swing by at eight. If you're outside we'll pick you up, if not, we'll leave you be. I hope that you'll come." He puts the baby in a football hold and walks me to the door. I turn to say goodbye before I descend the steps.

"Thanks for everything. I mean it. It's been a long time since I've been able to relax and let go."

"We'll walk you home. He should learn from a young age that you should always walk a woman to her door."

We walk down the steps and stroll over to Shady Lane. We arrive at door number three much too soon. I slip the key into the lock and open the door. Looking over my shoulder, I see Zane look at me with intensity.

"Can I kiss you again?" he asks.

"I wish you would," I reply. In fact, I really hope that he kisses me soon and often.

Chapter Seven

The early morning light almost blinds me as I step out of my room. Dressed in shorts and a T-shirt, I'm ready to get this run started. I look across the street and wait for the boys to emerge.

I see the single front wheel of the stroller appear. Zane looks both directions before he darts across the road. He's also dressed in shorts and a T-shirt. He has nice-looking legs—muscular calves and thighs as thick as tree trunks.

"Hi," I say as he approaches me.

"Hey there," he replies. He leans over and kisses my cheek. "Are you ready to run? I'll take it easy on you. Let's run into town and have breakfast, and then we can walk back. That should get us back in time to shower, and open the bar."

"You're on, if I make it the whole way without stopping, you have to buy me breakfast. If I stop along the way, you still have to buy because you got me up early to run."

He shakes his head and laughs. "Let's go. I was buying anyway."

We begin our run with a soft, easy jog, after warming up we fall into a steady rhythm. Our steps synchronize so that we are completely in line with one another. I'm breathing hard, and he's barely panting. My breathing evens out after a few minutes. We make it midway into town before we turn the corner and stop at the diner.

He reaches in and picks up the baby, leading us to a booth in the center of the room. Aaron is awake and happy. His little arms move spastically as his dad places him on the seat next to him. Zane is so careful with his son. I watch as he strategically places his hand next to the baby so there is no way he can take a tumble.

The waitress brings our menus along with glasses of ice-cold water. I drink deeply, trying to replace the moisture that I sweat away. Looking over my glass I take a peek at the man sitting across from me. His eyes are lowered as he looks over the menu. A bead of sweat is beginning to run down his forehead. I have the biggest urge to reach over and wipe it off.

"What are you looking at?" He raises his eyes and gazes toward me.

"I was just looking at you. You're pretty nice to look

at. You have this baby face and this tough-as-nails demeanor. They are in stark contrast to one another. I've had the pleasure of getting to know you the last few days. I've discovered that the gruff attitude is just a facade to throw people off. You're actually a really nice man."

"I can be a real jerk at times. I don't have a lot of tolerance for people who mistreat other people. I have zero tolerance when it comes to people messing with women and children."

"Do you think that comes from something or have you always been protective of women and children?"

"I imagine it comes from the respect I have for my mother, and what she had to do to raise three kids after my dad abandoned us. I also belonged to a biker group that is dedicated to helping children."

The waitress approaches our table to take our order. I ask for a ham and cheese omelet with fruit on the side. She looks to Zane, and he orders a veggie omelet, with a side of bacon, wheat toast, and a glass of milk.

"I saw your leather vest in the closet. What does BFK stand for?" I have been waiting for a chance to ask him about it, but I didn't want to admit that I was snooping in his closet.

"It stands for Bikers For Kids. We do a lot of

fundraising for children's charities, mostly we raise money for disadvantaged children, abandoned children, and children of abuse. I love kids, and I don't ever want to see a kid not get what they need, especially if I can contribute in some way. What are you passionate about?"

What am I passionate about? I love men who want to protect children. He's obviously a passionate man. He's big and strong, but tender enough to let a child melt his heart. Who wouldn't love that? I need very little time to ponder his question. My passions fall right in line with his.

"I love kids, too. I write software for kids and put it up on Freeware. I like to make games where kids think they're playing, but they are actually learning. You can learn a lot from playing the right kind of video game. I make things for all age groups. For younger kids, I start with things like colors and shapes. For older kids, I tend to write games that require critical thinking skills."

"I love that. I want to play some of your games. What platform can I use to play them?"

"Your PC will work just fine. I can help you download one of them if you would like me to."

I smile in his direction. I feel happy knowing that he appreciates what I do. I never had a lot of support from Tyler.

"Is that what you love to do—make games?" His eyes lift in question, and I wonder if maybe he doesn't appreciate it after all. Maybe he thinks it's silly.

"I do. I love creating something that isn't what it seems. I never really fully embraced the dream. My ex-husband wasn't supportive. He thought it was a child's fantasy. After several years of his haranguing, I gave up the dream and began coding for businesses like Lone Star—a tax software company." I look out the window and wonder what he's thinking. "I also have a contract with a space technology company. They often need navigation software for the satellites they produce. I like doing that, although, I probably won't hear from them again since I was referred by my father, and we are estranged."

His eyes shoot up at the word estranged. He looks like he is going to say something, but the waitress interrupts our conversation when she delivers our meal. Zane reaches down and rubs the head of his son. He is such a contented little man. We eat in silence but move into conversation halfway through.

"It's none of my business," he begins, "but I have to know. Your ex seems like an asshole. What was the attraction?"

"Do you have an hour or two?" I quip.

"I have all the time you need. I'm a very good listener." He takes a drink of his milk and puts the glass firmly back on the table. "You obviously have some deep-seated hurt, or you wouldn't be having nightmares about him."

I take a bite of fruit and stall. I don't know where to begin. I start my story of how Tyler and I met, and how he won my parents over and go from there.

"It was like he sprinkled magic powder over all of us, and we were under his spell. My parents were completely over the moon in love with him."

"What made him so special to your parents?"

"Honestly, I don't know. I think it's because my dad finally found the son he wanted. My mother was excited because she saw someone who could take over the business. She wanted my dad to spend more time living than working."

"How long did you date before he proposed?"

I think about Tyler's proposal and begin to laugh awkwardly.

"It wasn't so much of a proposal, as it was a merger. We went out to dinner, and he placed the box on the table. I opened it and saw a ring. He never said will you marry me, he just said, I think your mom has it all planned."

"Did she? Did she have your future planned?" He looks down at the baby and then back at me.

"Yes, I was married two months later. The wedding happened so fast that people expected me to show up in maternity wear."

"Why did you allow that to happen? I realize that hindsight is always 20/20, but we're talking about marriage and a lifetime commitment. You seem so strong and self-confident. Did the loss of control not bother you?" He takes the last bite of his omelet and sets his plate aside. He is completely focused on me.

"How is Aaron doing?" I try to deflect his attention to the baby.

"He's sleeping. Answer the question."

"You don't have to bully me to get an answer. I'll answer anything you want to know," I grumble.

"Good, I have lots of questions."

"In hindsight, I got caught up in the excitement. My mother was like a tsunami as far as planning goes. I got caught up in her wave." I push my plate aside and continue. "We all played our parts in this disaster. My mom wanted a wedding, my dad wanted a son, Tyler wanted access to everything he couldn't get on his own, and I wanted to please everyone."

"Did you love Tyler?" His eyes narrow as he stares at me.

"I loved the idea of Tyler. "I loved the picture-perfect boyfriend he bestowed upon me those first few months of dating. I didn't know or love the Tyler he became after we married."

"What do you mean?" He lifts Aaron up and puts him on his shoulder. The baby squirms and falls back to sleep.

"On our honeymoon, we took a three-week world tour. My husband spent most nights at the bar. I spent most nights in bed alone. He adopted a sex on Wednesday rule. He told me since it was known as "hump day" it would be our designated date night."

"So you're telling me that he had this amazingly sexy woman in his bed, and spent his nights at the bar, then refused to have sex on any other night but Wednesday?"

"Yep, that pretty much sums it up." Oh my God, did he just say I was sexy? Really?

"He sounds gay." My mouth drops open and my eyes grow big. How is this man so perceptive? "No fucking way. He is gay, isn't he?"

I want to laugh, and I want to cry. This is such a soap opera. I can hardly believe it's my life.

"Yep."

"When did you find out?" He reaches out one hand, and touches mine. His soft caress gives me courage to continue.

"Unfortunately, I never realized until the end. I wanted everything to be perfect, and so in my mind I made it perfect. I made excuses for his lack of interest. I made up reasons for why he slept in a different room. He was comfortable to be around—like a girlfriend."

"Was he…" he looks uncomfortable, "was he having sexual relations with others while he was married to you?"

The waitress approaches and asks if we need anything else. When Zane nods no, she leaves the bill on the table. He pulls out a twenty, places it on top of the ticket. We stand up to leave. I'm relieved to be going. The rest of this conversation is best held out of earshot of the general public.

We make sure Aaron is buckled into his stroller safely, and begin to walk back.

"You don't have to tell me the answer to my previous question. I realize that the subject is very personal." He pushes the stroller with one hand and holds my hand with the other. Holding his hand is such a natural thing to do. Telling him my secrets seems right, too.

"I'm okay with telling you. I don't know why, but I

feel safe with you. Am I wrong to feel safe? I'm obviously not a good judge of character, and I don't want my trust to be misplaced."

"You can trust me, Alexa. I'm not going to hurt you." He gives my hand a squeeze.

"I appreciate that. I don't think I could survive another heartbreak."

"You were railroaded into marrying that douche bag." Zane stops and turns to me. I watch as he takes my face into his hands. "You're a good person, and I feel something for you. I feel protective of you. I care about you." His lips consume mine. The whole world stops when he kisses me. I can't hear the traffic as it passes; I only hear the rush of blood as it travels to my brain. He pulls away from me, grabs my hand and we continue to walk.

"I care about you, too." I lace my fingers in his and squeeze. "Just in case you were wondering, I have been tested for HIV several times since my divorce." I don't look at him as I speak. I'm afraid to see something in his eyes. Will he be disgusted? I know I was, and then I was just scared shitless.

"I have to be honest. I was curious, but I never would have asked you. Now that you brought it up, weren't you furious? He exposed you to his lifestyle, and didn't give you the chance to protect yourself."

"I went through every emotion. I felt angry at his betrayal. I felt relieved that it wasn't me who kept him out of our bed, but his preference for men. I was scared he'd exposed me to AIDS, or something else. I was elated when my tests came back negative. My emotions ran the gamut."

"He is the worst type of man. He's a disgrace to the male population." I look around and see that we are more than halfway there. "What was his end game?"

"He was after my dad's business. He worked his way into a partnership, and when he got it, he let the pieces fall where they would. My dad lost half his company, and Tyler left a very wealthy man."

"Money— he ruined your life and your parents' lives, because he wanted money?" I look over at him and see the veins of his neck bulge. His face is red and it's not from the rising sun. He's angry.

"That pretty much sums it up. He is way worse than what you've heard, but I think that's all I can stomach for one day. I wouldn't say he ruined my life. He did some horrific things; some things I can't talk about for my own sanity." I think back to our last day in court and silently curse him to hell. "However, I'm still here. I was derailed for nearly five years. The four years I was married to him, and the year it took to divorce him are all I'm willing to give up. It was a bump in the road, but I'm finally back on track."

I'm glad your bump in the road led you here, Alexa." He points down to the baby. "He's great company, but he's not much of a conversationalist." That makes me smile. Being with this man makes me happy.

We walk the rest of the way in silence. He walks me to my door and waits for me to unlock it.

"I'll see you at four." I wait by the door and hope that he'll at least give me a peck on the cheek. I know I'm being greedy, but God, don't I deserve something good for a change? I traversed through mountains of shit this last year and I just want something good for a moment.

"I don't want to rush you into anything. It would appear that you have had a lot to contend with this last year. If I'm adding to your stress, I can step back and give you some space." He looks past me, into my room and then directly into my eyes. "I just want to hold you and kiss you senseless though."

My heart leaps with joy at his confession. I pull on his waistband and drag him into my room. With his hand on the stroller, he drags it in with him. I take a peek at the sleeping baby. Zane and I fall onto my bed and laugh.

"That might be the nicest thing anyone has said to me in years. I know you have to go open the bar so instead of kissing me senseless, can you kiss me until I'm scatterbrained?"

Leaning on his elbow, he props himself up and looks at me. His fingers come up to push my sweaty tendrils away from my forehead. His thumb traces over my cheekbone. He is looking at me with soft eyes and parted lips.

"Alexa, I want to give this a chance. Our connection – it's real. Do you want the same thing?" He leans down to brush his lips against mine. It's a soft feather of a touch coming from a large burly man. He is a person of contradictions. Everything that's rough and bristly is softened by something else. "I don't want to start something and have you take off on the next full moon."

"I'm not a runner, Zane. I'm happy here, and I'll stay as long as I continue to be happy." It's the most honest answer I can give. I look into his eyes. There is a smile there, but then the softness hardens slightly. His cheeks appear stone-like as he clenches his jaw tightly.

"Give me your lips woman," he growls. His lips settle on mine softly but deliberately. He manages to coax his tongue inside my mouth. I taste him, and it's the sweetest flavor in the world. It reminds me of sugarcane.

I roll my body next to his, wanting to know what he would feel like beside me. His free hand slides down my back and settles on my hip. My heart beats out an erratic rhythm that makes me breathless.

He breaks the kiss and pulls in my lower lip for a not-so-gentle suck. I moan as everything comes alive in my body. It's been a long time since I've felt a pang of passion from being in a man's arms. Selfishly, I want to keep him here to see how fabulous he can make me feel.

The palm of his hand spreads across my butt. He grabs a hold of my bottom and pulls me against him. I can tell that he is just as affected by our kiss as I am.

Roughly ten minutes later and several gasps and groans, he rolls onto his back and breathes deeply.

"I feel like a teenager again. Any minute now, I'm sure my mom is going to rush in here and catch us." He pulls his hands to his face and rubs. "I have to go open the bar. I would love to stay here and kiss you all day, but I can't. I need a cold shower."

I roll over and rub my hand against his stomach and work my way up to his chest. I can feel the roughness of his hair through his thin cotton shirt. I love the feel of him under my fingers. How his breath hitches each time I slowly cross over his peaked nipples.

"I'll see you at four. Thanks for breakfast and thanks for talking with me." I push myself into a seated position. The change in altitude makes me dizzy, or maybe it's his kisses that make me feel woozy.

With a groan, he slowly rises and pulls me to my feet. I fall into his embrace and feel him kiss the top of my head. He leans down for a chaste peck on the lips and then he moves toward the door with the baby in tow. I watch as he pushes the stroller across the street and disappears around the back of the bar.

In a matter of days, this man has taken the scarred girl I was, and set free the woman that I am. In his eyes, I'm smart, sexy and beautiful, and he wants me.

Chapter Eight

The afternoon floats by. I spend several hours on my project before I step into the shower and wash my hair. I spend extra time drying my hair. I want to make sure it smells good and feels better.

I want to look super nice today. I slip on a sundress and a pair of ballet flats. I pull my hair back in a pretty ribbon and apply my makeup. My swollen lips look luscious coated in a tinted gloss.

I look at the clock and see it's three-thirty. I pace the room waiting for the minute hand to move forward. The damn thing seems to be stuck. Why is it when you are looking forward to something, time stands still?

I force myself to wait another ten minutes before I shamelessly give in and head to the bar. I can hear the jukebox before I enter. Bon Jovi's "Livin on a Prayer" is playing. I slowly open the door and walk in. The dim lighting of the bar requires a minute for my eyes to adjust. I'm looking for one person and one person only—him. I scan the perimeter of the room and see him standing next to a table. His eyes turn toward me. We connect and the entire room of people fades away. He's dressed in jeans and a button-down shirt. I scan his body and see that he's upped his game tonight. A collared, button-down shirt is dressing up when it comes to Sugar Glen.

I slip past him and go behind the bar to pick up my apron. It's been washed; it almost looks new. I wrap the tie around my waist and fasten it behind my back.

Grabbing the tray from behind the bar, I stroll through the tables and pick up empties. As I walk past Zane, his hand slips out and grabs me. With his arm around my waist, he pins me next to him.

"Alexa, this is my good friend Dale," he says as he grips my waist.

"Nice to meet you, Dale." Dale is a nice-looking guy with black hair that is graying at the sides. He offers his hand in a gesture of welcoming. I reach for it and find my hand being pulled to his lips. Zane's body tenses, then relaxes as my hand is returned.

"Where did you find this beauty, Z?"

"I found her on the side of the road. She was in a heap of sweat and tears next to an old broken down, piece-of-shit car. I swooped her up and haven't let her out of my sight since."

"Is that right? I can't say I blame you." Dale smiles up at me.

"She thinks she is here just waiting for her car to be fixed, but I'm trying to convince her to give Sugar Glen a try."

Dale gives Zane one of those man looks that says *don't bullshit me, man.* His eyes roll as he says, "It's more like you want her to give you a chance."

"Well, I can't argue with that. I like her and I want her to stay."

"I hate to leave your little party, but I think I'll go pick up glasses while you two plan my future. It's nice to meet you, Dale."

I make the rounds and clean up what I can. My eyes keep straying to him and when I'm not looking for him, I am gazing up the stairs. I didn't really get to hold Aaron today, and I miss feeling him in my arms.

"You can go up and see him," the voice behind me says. He came up behind me so quietly I didn't realize he was there. I turn around quickly and find my face planted into his broad chest.

"You scared me. I was deep in thought." I step back and look up at him. His face is clean-shaven. I can smell the shaving cream and something else. "Are you wearing cologne?"

"Yes, I thought I would try to smell like something other than sweat and baby puke today. Do you like it?"

I inhale his scent and fake a swoon. "Why, Mr. Abbamonte, I do believe you smell delicious." I say in a very bad southern belle-esque manner.

A glorious smile spreads across his face. He turns me toward the stairs and gives me swat on my back end. "Go up and see my baby. He will be thrilled with your visit. If he's awake, bring him downstairs if you want. I can't have my patrons thinking what you did. It never occurred to me that I was giving off any kind of impression."

"Oh, you give off an impression all right—pure male—all sex." Shocked at the thought that just popped out of my mouth, I blush. I have to be the shade of a ripe strawberry.

"Glad I'm giving you the right impression. I would hate to mislead *you* in any way."

He's flirting—openly. I swing around and march back to him.

"I feel you—felt you. I know what impression you left on me. I'm looking forward to exploring that more." I'm shameless today. "I'm going up to visit my little man. Is it the redhead or the blonde upstairs?"

"It's the blonde."

"Hannah, okay I just wanted to know whom I was walking in on."

"Wait…her name is Hannah? I thought she was Ashley. I swear she said her name was Ashley."

I laugh as I walk away. It takes a few seconds before it registers with him. I walk up the stairs and hear him laugh.

Opening the door slowly, I peek in. I don't want to scare the poor girl.

"Hello," I whisper, not wanting to wake the baby if he's asleep.

"Hey," the blonde says as she trots over to the door. *Oh to have that kind of energy.* Baby Aaron is in her arms.

"I came up to get the baby. Zane wants me to bring him downstairs for a few minutes." She gives me a squinted, *I don't believe you* look.

"He's never brought the baby downstairs."

"Well, that's what he wants, so if you would like, you can bring him downstairs. I will take him from you then, and you can have a little break." I can see why she would be skeptical. This isn't the normal routine. I could tell her the truth, but I don't want to embarrass her by saying that he wants to make sure no one in the bar thinks he's bangin' the babysitter.

She pulls the baby close to her chest and begins to walk down the steps. I like the way she holds him tightly and takes the steps carefully. She is carrying precious cargo.

I follow right behind her. I want to get my hands on that baby before everyone else in the bar loses their minds over him.

At the bottom of the steps is Zane. He looks at Ashley and then at me. I shrug my shoulders. I know he's wondering why I didn't bring him down. He holds out his arms and takes the baby.

"Ashley, go tell Bud what you want to eat. Alexa and I have it under control."

As she saunters to the kitchen, he hands me the baby. I pull him up to my face and nuzzle his neck. I breathe deeply trying to suck in his sweet baby goodness. What is it about babies and puppies that make them smell so good?

"So, do you want him back, or can I have him for a minute?"

"He's all yours, sweetie. Why don't you take him around and introduce him to some of the regulars? I used to have him down here in a bassinet before I hired a bevy of girls to watch him."

I'm so excited to show him off. He's not mine, but I think he's the cutest baby on the planet.

Aaron gets passed from person to person. I stand close by making sure to take him back if needed. I look toward Zane and he's watching us both protectively. No matter where I go his eyes track me. I'm sure it's because he is hyper aware of his son's location, but I like the feeling of his eyes on me.

Aaron lets out a displeased scream. He's had enough shuffling between people for the day. Out of nowhere comes Ashley to swoop in, and spirit him upstairs. I kind of feel jealous of her. She gets to feed and change his diapers and I get to serve beer and stare at the beautiful man behind the bar. Well, I guess I can't be too jealous. My view isn't too shabby.

The night passes by swiftly. For a Tuesday, it seems pretty busy to me. I find every reason I can, to go behind the bar. He seems to find every reason to touch me in some way. He holds my hip as he passes by. He glides his hand across my arm when I stand next to him. Each touch ignites a fire inside me. I don't know when the last time I felt this charged by a touch. It's the possibilities that his touch implies.

I close the door after the last patron leaves, sliding

the deadbolt into its place. I hear the jukebox begin to play the classic sound of The Police. I recognize the song immediately as "Every Breath You Take."

He slides up behind me and slips his arms around me, pulling my back to his chest. I lean against him and melt into his embrace. This is where I've wanted to be all evening. His song choice doesn't go unnoticed.

We rock back and forth as the music plays softly throughout the empty bar.

"I didn't tell you earlier, but you look beautiful tonight."

His lips gently caress my neck. He hits that perfect spot where the neck and shoulder connect. The goose bumps rise on my flesh as his mouth follows my collarbone to my shoulder. I lean my head to the other side giving him unfettered access. I feel his chin rest in the crook of my neck.

His hips push forward, forcing me to adopt his rhythm. As he sways in each direction, I follow as if my body is glued to his. I hear him hum along with the song, and I am lost in the moment. His hands travel from my hips up my sides, slowing down as he passes the rise of my breasts. It wasn't a feel exactly, just a soft caress as he pulls his hands to my shoulder. A shiver of excitement runs down my spine.

"Are you cold?" he asks.

I giggle a bit knowing that my shiver has nothing to do with the temperature of the room and everything to do the temperature of my core. He has managed to set my senses on fire once again.

"No, I'm not cold, I just got a chill from your touch. It was nice."

"Touching you is nice. I like it so much that I wish I could do it all night. However, I have to let the sitter go. I just wanted to have at least one dance with you before the night was over."

I turn around and face him. I don't want the night to be over, but I know he needs to get upstairs.

"We didn't clean up, I still need to sweep," I say looking up to him. I can't take my eyes off his lips. I know what they feel like and I want to feel them all over me.

"I can get it tomorrow. You must be tired, I got you up early for a run."

"I feel pretty good, although my legs hurt. Are we going tomorrow morning?" I ask with hope.

"No, I have to take Aaron to see my mom. Do you want to come? I can pick you up at the same time, only this time we'll drive."

Without thinking I blurt, "Yes, I would love to come. I'll be ready."

We walk slowly to the door, his hand is wrapped around my waist guiding me. I stop and wait for him to slide the deadbolt. He pulls my chin up with two fingers and settles his soft lips against mine. For a man his size, he can have such a gentle touch. I fall into the kiss right away. I need no coaxing to open my lips. I'm begging him to invade me. I want him to control me. I give myself freely.

He pulls away with a groan and slips the bolt aside. The harsh sound brings me out of my Zane-induced trance.

"I'll be out front at eight. I usually stop by the donut shop on the way to pick up Mom's favorites. I'll buy breakfast again."

"Okay," I say softly, still reeling from the effects of his kiss. I walk in a dream-like state across the street and back to my room. Looking over my shoulder I see him watch me. He won't leave until he knows that I'm safely inside. Just before I close the door, I blow him a kiss.

Chapter Nine

Eight o'clock would usually be an ungodly time for me to be ready. I'm more of a sleep-in kind of girl. I love working as a consultant, doing bit jobs. I get to choose my own hours. Having said that, I would have been up and ready at three in the morning if that's what time he said he was picking me up.

I misjudged him and if I had bolted after I got a dose of who I thought he was, I would have missed out on something wonderful.

I hear the crunch of gravel in front of my room. Like a teenager, I jump up and down at the thought of seeing him again. I check myself in the mirror and pick up my bag from the dresser before I dash out the door.

A silver sedan has pulled up in front of my room. I don't recognize the car, but I know the driver well. I pull open the door before he can exit. He looks sexy as hell in his polo shirt and shorts.

"Hey," I say as I hop in the passenger side.

"Hey, yourself," he replies as he leans over to kiss

me. "I would have come to your door to get you."

"I know, but the baby is in the car, and I was excited about seeing you both." I turn to the back seat and see that the car seat is securely fastened in a rear-facing position. "Whose car is this?" I ask, having never seen it before.

"It's mine. I bought it when I picked him up from San Francisco. I didn't want him to ride in the front of the truck. I had no idea how to fly with an infant, so, we had our first road trip together on his second day of life."

"You totally amaze me. I had you pegged so wrong. I'm sorry for judging you."

"You judged me? I'm shocked," he jokes. "I deserved your initial opinion, I was surly and impatient. I apologize."

"You are forgiven."

"On second thought, I don't think I'm going to let you off that easy," he responds. "I'm thinking that I can probably forgive you if you say yes to a date on Monday night."

"Do I have to wait until Monday for more kisses? If that's the case, the answer is no. I'd rather not be forgiven at all. You can punish me with your mouth." *Did I just say that? What the hell has gotten into me?*

He raises an eyebrow at me. "Tell you what, I will

131

take you on that date, but until then I will punish you with lots of kisses." He puts the car in gear and backs out.

Twenty minutes later, we arrive at the home where his mother lives. Zane has the baby and I have the baby bag and donuts. It's a lovely place. It looks like a regular apartment complex, but there are a lot of staff members on hand. The grounds are beautiful—full of rose bushes and lush green trees.

Everyone seems to know Zane. As we walk through the entry, he is greeted by name. I swear all the women come up to see the baby. At least that's what they are pretending to do. I'm a woman, so I know how this works. You pretend to be interested in the baby, but actually it's the father you want to see. I watch as the women put their hands on his back as if that's going to help them see the baby better. I stand off to the side and take it all in.

He is friendly to the staff but keeps his eye on me. I can see the pleading look, something that says *save me*.

I walk up to the crowd and whisper into his ear. "Should I take Aaron to see your mom while you take care of your harem?" His eyes shoot to mine with what looks like shock. I wonder what he's thinking. If he's wondering if I'm jealous, then he's right. These women have their hands all over what I feel is mine. I have no claim to him, but I don't like watching them feel him up either.

"Sorry, ladies but we have to take this little guy to see my mom. Oh, and, by the way, for those of you who haven't met Alexa, she's my girlfriend, and you'll probably be seeing a lot more of her." He looks at me and smiles. "Honey, can you take the baby for a minute?" he asks. My eyes shoot up to his. I'm surprised at his declaration. I happily trade him my packages for the baby. I cuddle Aaron up to my neck while he coos. *He called me his girlfriend.* We walk away, I turn to look over my shoulder and see the looks of many disappointed women.

I follow him down the corridor and up to door number fifteen. He pushes the bell and we wait.

"You just crushed the hopes of the entire population of single women in Sugar Glen," I tease.

"I saw the look on your face as they rushed up to see the baby. You tried to slink into the background. You are no one's background, Alexa."

I've lived in the background for years. His statement pulls me into the forefront, the center of his universe and I feel special. "I appreciate that, but you didn't need to publicly declare me as your girlfriend. I love that you did, but I have no claim on you." I nuzzle my nose into the soft folds of Aaron's neck.

"That's where you're wrong. You gripped my heart the first time you kissed me, and every time you press your lips to mine, I get a little tighter squeeze right here." He claps his free hand against his heart.

I look up at him with so many questions in my head. I open my mouth to ask him if he's lost his mind, but I'm disrupted by the sound of the deadbolt sliding open.

On the other side of the door is a small woman. She stands maybe five foot three or so, but not much taller. Her bright red hair is a stark contrast to her pale complexion. Her eyes are a blue-green hazel. They light up like a fluorescent bulb as soon as she sees the baby in my arms.

She moves to the side and lets us enter. I watch as she shuffles her feet. Zane reaches down to give his mother a hug.

"Mom, this is Alexa." I shift the baby into one arm so that I can offer her my hand. She raises her shaking palm to grab mine, and squeezes. "This is my mom, Elaine." I smile at his mom. She waves for us to follow. We line up and shuffle behind her until we reach her living room. It's a beautiful space. She has plush furniture with dark wood accents. I would say it's an odd mix between Tuscan and mission, but it works. It feels homey and comfortable.

She points me to the loveseat and sits next to me, no doubt because she wants to see the baby. I hold him out to her, and watch as her face falls.

"She's afraid to hold him. She thinks she is going to drop him," Zane says. The sadness is evident in his voice.

"That's crazy talk," I say as I look between the two of them. "Go grab me a few towels or some pillowcases." I must have sounded like I meant business because Zane jumped to my bidding right away. It was kind of funny to see him pop up after my command. I'm usually the one hopping when he barks out orders.

"Ii…it's ooook-ay," his mom slurs. She places her hand on my knee and gives it a gentle pinch.

"No, it's not," I say. "A grandmother should be able to hold her grandbaby. It's the benefit of having raised your own children." I smile warmly at her. Zane approaches with several pillowcases. I take them all, and find the oldest in the bunch.

"Can I tear this one?" I hold up the blue one with the frayed corners. "I will replace it the next time I visit." I look to Zane for permission as he turns to his mother. I follow his eyes and watch as she nods yes.

Handing the baby off to his dad, I grip the frayed corner and tear. I do the same at the other end. I am left with a strip of fabric that is about five-feet long and almost two-feet wide. I stand up and wrap the swath of fabric around Elaine's neck. When I get the length just about right, I tie the ends to make a sling. I ask her to sit back and relax. I don't want the weight of the baby to pull on her neck. Once she is situated, I take Aaron back into my arms and slide him into the sling. His weight forces the fabric to cup on the sides, creating a cradle of sorts. He squirms a bit, but settles comfortably in what I would call a baby hammock. I grab the throw pillow from the corner of the couch and wedge it under her arm to help support Aaron's weight. Pleased with my work, I step back and watch.

Elaine's eyes pool with tears as she looks down at the baby in her arms. Her hands are free to investigate his fingers and toes. I watch as she holds him for what I assume is the first time. Knowing that it's probably close to feeding time, I nudge Zane toward the baby bag hoping that he'll figure it out.

He's a sharp one, that man. He pulls the premade bottle out of the bag and hands it to his mother. I wish I had a camera to capture this moment.

I walk over to the larger sofa and sit. Sometimes the

biggest problems have the simplest solutions. He sits by his mother and guides her shaking hand to the baby's mouth. As soon as he latches onto the nipple, the bottle becomes stable. Pure joy exudes from every pore of her body. All of her attention is focused on the little man she holds. The big man rises and comes to sit next to me.

"You're amazing. Look at her. She's feeding my son. I don't think she ever thought it was possible. You show up, tie a few pieces of fabric together and it all becomes real." His hand rests on my bare knee. "Thank you."

"You're welcome. My mom made me something similar when I was going through a baby-wearing phase in my youth. She got tired of me handing her my doll after I grew weary of carrying it around. It's a simple concept." I glance over at her feeding the baby and smile. "They both seem very happy. The baby is getting what he wants, and your mom is getting what she needs—to feel like a grandma."

He moves his hand up to my shoulder, pulling me into the side of his body. His lips press into the top of my head. His mother gazes up at us and smiles. I'm not sure if her smile is from holding her grandchild, or seeing her son with me. Either way, my heart is warmed knowing I was able to help in some small way.

We spend the next hour watching Elaine fuss over the little one in her lap. Looking at his watch, Zane tells her that he needs to get back to open the bar. Reluctantly she releases the baby. I pack up his bag and wait. Elaine reaches out her hand to me. I take it and press her fingers gently between mine. She tugs me into an embrace and whispers in my ear, "Thank you." Her voice sounds stronger. It's as if holding her grandbaby was therapeutic.

"We'll see you on Friday, Mom. I love you." He leans in and gives his mom a kiss on the cheek. He stays for a minute longer as if he's listening to something. "I will, Mom. Have a great day."

We walk out the way we came. The day seems a bit brighter.

"We never ate the donuts, I still owe you a meal. Come over to the bar and I will cook you brunch."

"That's okay, I have food at home." I tell him as I watch him strap his child safely into the seat. I don't think I have ever seen a man pay such close attention to every detail as Zane does when it comes to his son.

"Your mom is lovely." I climb into my seat and buckle up as I'm talking. He is already in the driver's seat ready to go. "She really enjoyed feeding the baby."

"I don't think I've seen her that happy in a long time.

138

You did something wonderful today. Did you see the light in her eyes when Aaron was in her lap and she was able to feed him?"

"I'm glad I could help," I say sheepishly. I'm not used to this much praise in one day. In one month really.

"You changed her life forever. She told me before we left it was her best day in a long time, and to make sure I keep you. She expects to see you Friday." He reaches over and holds my hand. "Will you come with me on Friday?"

"Of course I'll come, who is going to tie the pillowcases?" I tease. "However, I want my donut next time." Our fingers intertwine like braided ribbon. The heat from his hand runs up my arm to warm my heart.

"That's an impossibility, Fridays are breakfast sandwiches and coffee."

"Oh…I'm not sure then. If I have to settle for breakfast sandwiches, then I'm going to need something else to sweeten the pot."

"Now you're getting greedy. I'll see what I can come up with to sweeten the deal."

Before I realize it, we are back to our side of town. He pulls up in front of my room and parks. Racing to my side of the car, he swings open the door and helps me out. I take his hand as he pulls me out of my seat and into his arms. I crumble against his warm chest. He lifts me up onto my tiptoes and kisses me senseless.

"I expect to see you at the bar in an hour or less. Bring your computer. You can work from there. I'll clean out a quiet corner for you."

"No, it's okay. I'll work here."

He sets me down and looks at me sternly.

"Alexa, I'm not asking you. I'm telling you to be at the bar within an hour." He leans over and gives me sweet little peck on the lips. "I want to feed you so you don't eat some microwave shit from a can."

He turns away from me, hops in the car, and drives away. I stare after him and wonder if people buy into this bossy side of him. It doesn't matter that he is bossy. It doesn't matter that we have only kissed and not taken things further. In fact, it makes it all the sweeter as he has helped me feel good about myself. I feel validated, as if my ideas are gold. I felt accepted when his mom held me close and showed me how much she cared that I had come. I felt cherished when he told me I was no one's background. This man is much more than I originally thought, and I feel so thankful that he picked me up that day.

Against my better judgment, I pack up my computer and head on over to Last Resort. Actually, Last Resort is the first place I want to be.

Chapter Ten

True to his word, Zane cleared off the table in the corner. He poured me a Diet Coke and told me he asked Bud to make me bacon, eggs and toast. It's not Bud's usual fare, so I'm wondering how good it can be. Can he even cook an egg? He looks more like a burger and fry guy.

Fifteen minutes later, he delivers my meal and joins me. I guess Bud is a master at everything. The eggs are cooked perfectly, the bacon crisp, and the toast lightly browned.

"Tell me what you're working on," he says as he dips his toast into the creamy golden yolk.

"It's boring really, but the long and short of it is that this tax software is supposed to take you to different windows when you finish entries and it's failing to do that. It's also using wrong tax percentages. It's not a big fix, in fact, I thought it would take me weeks, but I think I will have it done in a few days." I pick up a piece of bacon and savor the salty crunch.

"Todd called me since he didn't have your number.

He left a message at the motel. He wanted me to tell you that your car would be finished today. He is going to drop it off at the motel and bring you the keys."

"Wow, that was quick. I thought he wouldn't have it fixed until Friday."

"I guess it was a slow week at the shop." He glances up at me and I see something in his eyes. Is it sadness or concern?

"Do you mind if I stick around for a while longer? I'd like to keep my job for a bit and see if Sugar Glen is actually really sweet. This gruff man told me when I arrived in town to not be fooled by the name. I've come to like it here, and want to feel it out a bit before I make a hasty decision to leave."

His smile starts small and broadens with every word. He bolts off his seat and grabs some type of paper from behind the counter. I look down and see a W-4 Form.

"You will have to fill one of these out. Since you are a permanent employee, I can invest a little more money in you. I require a year's notice when you quit." He can't keep a straight face.

"I'll take what you're paying me now, and if I decide to leave, I will give you a two-week notice."

"Hmm...I'll pay you more, and we will negotiate

later if you ever want to leave."

"All right, now eat and leave me alone, I have to finish this if I want to get paid." I fill out a W-4 Form while I finish my meal. I pass it over to my sexy-as-sin boss and focus on the task at hand.

"Your birthday is in two weeks. Let's plan something special. How about we go on a date?"

"A date? That's the second date you have asked me on today. Do you realize that if you continue to be so sweet, the gruff disposition you try to pass off as your norm isn't going to be believable?" I tilt my head and smirk in his direction. "Why is it that you act so surly, when you're just a big teddy bear?"

"I am surly. Don't think because I've been what you would consider sweet, a sign of softness. I'm far from being a pushover, and I like to control everything around me." Is that a warning, or he is just trying to re-establish his authority?

"Go away. You wanted me here. I'm doing what you wanted, now leave me be so I can work." He picks up our plates and begins to walk toward the kitchen. He gets a few steps away and turns on his heel, comes back, and gives me a kiss.

"I'm just trying to sweeten the pot. You seem to have

swindled more kisses out of me."

"Are you saying that you don't want to kiss me? Is this your way of getting me to go to your mother's Friday to tie the pillowcases?"

"I have to use anything I can, to get my way. Is it working?"

"Kiss me again, I need a sweeter pot. Then go away and leave me alone."

He puts the plates down and pulls me into a kiss. His soft, sweet, tongue dances with mine. He pulls away, leaving me breathless, and wanting more—so much more.

I keep busy on my coding, and finish what I had planned just in time for my shift to start. It's a slow Wednesday night at the bar. I spend the extra time staring at Zane and trying to figure him out. I saunter over to the bar and sidle up to him. How has he managed to stay single? It's not as if the women aren't falling all over him wherever we go. More importantly, how did I ever catch his eye?

"What's your story? Why is a good-looking guy like you single?"

"I'm not. I have a smokin' hot girlfriend that I found on the side of the road. She lives in this dumpy motel across the street from me and has a penchant for crappy canned foods."

I reach up and slug him in the arm. "Seriously, what is your story? I know why you came to Sugar Glen, but why are you single? What are you, like thirty?"

"Yep, I'm thirty. I had a girlfriend for a short time in California, but it didn't work out. She wasn't the one. It was good she was gone before I had to come here." He looks around the bar. "She would have never been able to survive in this little Podunk town. She was high maintenance and low tolerance." He laughs to himself. "I can't imagine what she would have said if I had a child. I don't think she liked kids. She acted too much like one to want one."

"That's too bad. What attracted you to her?" I'm curious what would make this man, date a girl that sounds like a nightmare.

He gives me that, *are you really going to ask me that* look.

"What do you think I was attracted to? I liked her for her brain of course." He shakes his head and walks away.

I pick up the wet dishrag and throw it at him. He catches it mid-air and in less than five steps he is next to me. I am lifted off my feet and held up in the air.

"Did you just throw a dirty wet rag at me? You are in

so much trouble." He shifts my weight effortlessly so he is holding me with one arm around my thighs. My stomach is pressed against his face. I feel the first smack against my butt. It's playful, but I play along by squirming. I act as if I am fighting for my life.

"Bud!" I scream. "Bud, come and help me." Zane swats my bottom again. This time he lets his hand linger momentarily.

Bud runs out of the kitchen with his butcher knife in his hand. "What the hell is going on here?" he yells. He looks around at the empty room. "What the hell? I thought you were being mugged out here. Why don't you two just do it and get it over with." He shakes his head at us and walks back into his kitchen, grumbling the entire way.

"See, you're getting no help from Bud. I should take you upstairs and throw you over my knee."

I am so into that idea. He lets me slide down his body. His hands glide from my bottom to my shoulders as my breasts slide down his chest. The friction makes my nipples harden. The sweet sensation of arousal is an aphrodisiac.

I replay the scene in my head and begin to laugh. Watching Bud run out of the kitchen flailing a knife is funny. More importantly is his comment about going upstairs and doing it. Now, that statement has merit.

"I don't think Bud was suggesting a spanking," I tell him.

His lips crush mine. I pull my hands through his hair and hold him against me. I can feel his arousal press against my stomach. His hands reach down to my hips, He grasps both sides and pulls me into him.

Like a duet, we moan in unison. "Let's close the bar and go upstairs. We only have an hour left anyway. I'm sure Claire would love to leave early."

"Claire? Is she the redhead?" I think back to the one time I met her. I couldn't come up with a name for her.

"What did you name her?" He smirks at me as if he's expecting me to blurt out Annie or some crazy thing.

"I couldn't figure her out."

"Go and lock the door, I'll tell Bud we're closing for the night." He swats my butt as I turn around and head for the door.

With the bar closed up, he guides me up the stairs and into his home.

"Hey, Claire, you're out of here. I closed the bar early." He hands her a wad of twenties and walks her to the back door. He watches her until she is safely in her car.

As soon as he shuts the door, he closes in on me. I've

settled myself on the sofa. He wastes no time pinning my body under his. Hot lips run up my neck to nibble on my earlobe. I wonder if his heart is beating at the same rate as my own. There is no time to think while his lips rain kisses from my neck to my mouth. He pulls away and I feel the loss of his touch. I think I even whimpered out loud.

"This couch is not the place for this kind of activity. I have a bed." He winks at me as he pulls me into a sitting position. My feet slide to the ground and hit the floor with a thud. A groan escapes my lips as the pain radiates up my legs.

"Would you like a glass of wine, it might help you relax?" His eyes look into mine, they soften as he looks at me.

As much as I was about ready to strip the man down and climb him like a tree, a glass of wine actually sounds heavenly. I am tired. My feet are killing me, first from the run yesterday – note to self: running requires decent runners – and now from my shift. Zane keeps surprising me with his genteel kindness. Am I just not used to being treated like a lady anymore?

"Yes, that sounds great."

He brings two glasses of red wine with him and sits next to me.

"You look tired. Are you okay?" He places his hand on my thigh and rubs gently. My body tingles all over from his touch.

"My feet hurt, but I'm all right. It's nice to sit and relax."

He shifts his body and pulls my feet into his lap. He tosses off my shoes and rubs the tension from balls of my feet. After yesterday's run and standing on my feet during the shifts I've worked, my feet are killing me. I'm going to have to invest in a good pair of shoes. Focusing my attention on his ministrations, I fall back into the soft leather of the sofa and close my eyes.

"Hey, sweets…I ran you a bubble bath. Why don't you get undressed and climb in," he whispers in my ear. I didn't even realize I had fallen asleep. The last thing I remember was having my feet rubbed.

"Oh, I'm so sorry. I fell asleep on you. God, how awful." How could I do that? We finally had some time alone and I spent it sleeping. We were so close to doing the deed and I blew it.

"You were tired. Besides I liked watching you sleep."

He helps me up and walks me to the bathroom where a bubble bath beckons me. The smell of baby soap perfumes the air. On the ledge of the tub is a glass of wine.

"You are so sweet. I don't care what everyone else says." I walk in and turn around. I have no idea what I'm supposed to do. Is he joining me? Is he watching me?

"Yeah, well don't tell anyone. You know where the towels are located. I put a T-shirt on the counter for you. You can use my toothbrush if you like." He turns to leave.

"You're leaving me?"

"If I stayed, beautiful, you wouldn't be relaxing and I fear you would be twice as sore tomorrow." He brushes his lips against mine, and retreats.

What does that mean? I know what it implies but does that mean he wants me to stay the night? He did offer up his toothbrush and a T-shirt. Are we going to have sex? Do I want to have sex with him? *Uh-duh...of course you do,* my inner voice answers.

I'm not ready to have sex; I didn't shave my legs today. I undress and search his bathroom drawer for his razor. Once I find it, I slowly sink into the steaming tub and relax. The bubbles are soothing and the wine is making my tense muscles feel like jelly. I rapidly run the razor over my stubbly legs just in case. I toss back the remainder of my wine and let the water drain.

I could have stayed in his tub all night, but I don't want to waste my time on me when I can be with him.

I pull his T-shirt over my head and watch as it falls nearly to my knees. I'm not putting my dirty underwear back on, so it's commando for me tonight. Looking at his toothbrush, I contemplate whether or not to use it. I'm not sure we are at the place in our relationship where we can share a toothbrush. Isn't that too intimate? *You're thinking about letting him press himself inside of you, and now you're debating whether to let his toothbrush enter your mouth?* I laugh at how incredibly obtuse I'm being.

I quickly brush my teeth, brush my hair, and exit the bathroom.

The house is silent. I pad through the hallway and into the living room where I see him lying on the couch. Trying not to disturb him, I silently tiptoe to the chair that flanks the sofa.

"How was your bath?" The sound of his voice startles me. I jump what feels like several feet.

"You scared me. I thought you were sleeping." He leans forward and pulls me across his body. The T-shirt slips up and shows off my thighs. "The bath was wonderful. Thank you. I don't think anyone has ever run me a bath. I'm touched."

"Your ex is a dick." He pulls me down on top of his body. We lie with our stomachs pressed together and my head on his chest.

"Yes, he is." I move around until I feel comfortable. His hands rub my back in a slow and gentle up and down motion. His fingertips barely graze my naked thighs and bare bottom. I squirm trying to pull the T-shirt down to cover myself.

"Don't," he says calmly. "I can't see you, but I want to touch your soft skin. I'm not going to push you any further than you want to go. Lying here with you is perfect just as it is."

"I'm not worried about you pushing, Zane, I'm worried that you won't like me." Did I really just say that out loud? Was I this insecure before Tyler?

He stops everything and leans up to look into my eyes.

"How could I not like you? Even if I took the fact you're beautiful out of the equation, which I can't, you are still the nicest, kind-hearted girl I've ever met."

"You're just trying to get into my T-shirt," I tease.

"I bamboozled you into working with me, which I have to say is one of my finest moments. You look at my baby with the loving eyes of a parent. You treated my mom like she was important to you. How could I not *like* you?" He tweaks my chin. "Yes, you're right. I would love to get into your T-shirt, but just being with you is good enough for now. Will you spend the night? No expectations, I just want to hold you."

He just wants to hold you? Yeah, right. My subconscious is very vocal today. I snuggle my face into his chest and breathe. It feels so good to be here.

"Let's climb in bed, sweets. The baby will be up at some point tonight, and I want to snuggle before he interrupts our time together."

I lift myself from his chest, trying hard not to let the T-shirt ride up and show off the goods. Maybe my decision to not wear underwear wasn't well thought out. As soon as I'm in a standing position, he takes my hand and leads me to his bed. The comforter is already pulled to the end of the bed and a light blanket and sheet are all that remain.

I feel nervous. I'm about to climb into bed with this man, and I have no idea what to expect. I slide into his bed and pull the sheet over my body.

"Do you prefer a particular side?" I ask. I know that I tend to gravitate to the right side, but I can sleep just about anywhere.

"You're fine just where you're at." I lie back on the pillow and watch as he undresses.

He's obviously comfortable in his own skin. He pulls his shirt off like most men, crossing his arms in front and grabbing the hem to lift it over his head. I watch as his body is slowly revealed. It's like having my own Chippendale model right here. I see his happy trail emerge as the shirt slowly glides up his torso. Strong abs and a broad chest come into view. He tosses his shirt onto the dresser and reaches for the belt of his jeans. He pulls it free from his pants and rolls it up to sit next to his shirt. He unbuttons his jeans and pulls down the zipper. My breath catches as he steps out of his pants. His boxer briefs hug tightly to his thighs and show every muscle he has. He turns around and walks into the bathroom and I am gifted with a fantastic rear-end view.

He climbs into bed beside me, smelling of peppermint toothpaste. I snuggle up in the safety of his arms, knowing there is nowhere I would rather be. He pulls me close to his chest. The feeling of peace and safety pervades any other thought and I quickly fall asleep.

Chapter Eleven

I'm so hot, the sweat pours from my brow. So much pain—so much blood. Oh my God, no! No!

"Alexa! Wake up. Sweetie, you're okay. Wake up!"

My heart feels like it is pounding out of my chest. I feel hands on my shoulders shaking me gently. I swallow the panic as I realize it's a dream. I look around the room and realize that it's early morning. Zane looks at me with concern in his eyes.

"I'm sorry, you must think I'm insane." I reach up and hold on to Zane as if my life depended on it. "Hold me, please."

He lies down with me, wrapping me in his strong arms.

"Shhh, I don't think you're crazy, I think you're working through things. Do you want to talk about it?"

"No, I don't," I say softly, the last thing I want to do is relive the nightmare. What I want most is to forget it ever happened. I pull myself tightly against him, knowing in my heart that the warmth of his body will soothe my aching

156

soul. His strong arms embrace me. He holds me like one would hold a beloved child. One arm presses against my back while the other cradles my head against his chest.

His hand gently strokes my back. The strumming motion is like an elixir to my raw nerves. I relax completely under his loving ministrations. Wrapping his fingers through my hair, he gently pulls my head back giving him access to my lips.

His lips brush mine with uncertainty. I can feel his hesitation as his mouth barely glides across mine. I lean into the kiss, only to have him retreat. I tug my head forward, breaking his hold on my hair. I need his lips on mine.

Unrestrained, I crush my mouth into his. I feel like this kiss is just as important as my next breath. Without it, I may wither to nothing. I want to feel something other than pain and sorrow. *I need to feel love.*

"I need you to love me, Zane," I say into his mouth as I push the kiss deeper. Whatever reticence he was feeling disappears as his mouth covers mine in a heated kiss. He groans as he shifts his body, throwing one leg across my thigh. One of his hands lies beneath me, splayed across my back. The other hand begins to roam my body freely.

His hand slips beneath my shirt sending shivers down the length of my spine. I arch my back as his palm floats across the heated surface of my chest. I can feel my breasts harden and reach for his touch as he passes.

I hear another groan, but this one comes from deep inside me. The sound is breathy and throaty at the same time. I turn to my side and push my hips forward. I feel his arousal pushing against my thigh and shamelessly grind against him. If I could, I would crawl inside of him.

"I want you, Alexa. I want to make love to you, but I don't want it to be therapy for you. I want it to be something that's more than a quick fix." I look into his stormy eyes and see how the world should be. When a man looks at you in a pure and unfiltered way, it changes you.

"You stir things in me that make me want so much more than a quick fix. I want you. Everything about you calls to me in a profound and special way." I pepper his face with kisses. "I can't say that making love to you won't be healing for me. I can guarantee you that treatment is not why I would do it. I want to feel you move inside of me. I want to connect to you in a deeper, more meaningful way."

He gently pulls me away from his body and lays me down beside him. His hands caress me from top to bottom. The care with which he touches me is moving. I don't think

I've ever felt so desired.

"I want you to realize that if we do this, everything changes. I don't want you to sleep in the motel across the street. I want you sleeping with me." He presses his lips against mine in a completely possessive manner. He breaks the kiss to deliver a warning. "I don't know if you're ready to be with me. I have a child, and my life is messy at best."

It takes me just a second to ponder my choices. I can get up and walk away, but that would mean no Zane, or Aaron. I could stay and make love to this man, but that means that I have to expose myself to him completely.

Without a second thought I tell him, "I'm ready, Zane, life is messy. I know that for a fact. I'm not looking for neat and tidy. I'm looking for something real."

"Real, I can give you. Right now the realest thing I can offer is passion and desire."

He pushes himself next to me. There is no doubt he is feeling desire.

His hand runs up my stomach and lingers at my breasts. He draws soft swirls over and across the tender flesh. The sensation forces the breath from my lungs. I'm not a stranger to desire, only fulfillment.

"Before we start this, what's our timeline like? Where is the baby?" I can barely get the words out.

"I just put him back down, he'll be out for hours. What do you have in mind?" His brows rise in question.

"What are you offering?" I want to try everything with him. Anything he offers will outshine anything I've had.

"I'm offering it all. Let's go from A to Z. If that's not enough, we'll make shit up."

He peels off his briefs and focuses all of his attention on me. He slowly peels my shirt up, kissing the newly exposed flesh as he works the soft cotton inch by inch up my body. The hitch in his breath excites me as my shirt is pulled over my head. I look into his eyes and see unbridled desire. I've never been so aroused.

Every kiss he delivers is calculated and precise. The heat of his tongue burns straight to my core. His fingers dance across my body in a rhythm that he created for me alone. I've never had anyone worship my body before, but that's exactly what this feels like. He spends an inconceivable amount of time getting acquainted with every inch of me. I had no idea that lips could be so erotic when placed in the right place with the right pressure.

I try to reciprocate, but he lays me back and tells me that today is all about me. My mind goes blank as my body takes over.

He shifts his body, licking a trail from my ankle to my knee. Foreign sounds escape my lips. It's not until he settles between my legs that I realize he has no intention of hurrying his exploration.

My hips rise off the bed as soon as his lips meet my most sensitive area. The intensity and heat his tongue delivers leaves me breathless and desperate for release. He crawls up my body, settling himself between my legs. I'm quivering from the inside out. It's not going to take much to push me over the edge.

He covers himself with a condom that has appeared out of nowhere. With a gentle push, he enters me, and for the first time in years, I feel complete. I exhale and let him fill me with hope, love and him.

His steady rhythm takes my body to a place I've only dreamed about. I feel the tension begin at the base of my spine. My head feels woozy and wonderful. I inhale and hold my breath until dizziness threatens to consume me. I release the breath I've been holding, and let my body surge over the edge. Spasms wrack me as I clench tightly around him. I know the exact moment he finds his pleasure. He swells within me just before I feel his pulsing release. His eyes lock with mine, and I see my future in his passionate gaze.

The moment will be forever etched in my mind. My body hums with satisfaction. We lay sated in each other's arms. His breathing slows from erratic gasps to a steady even flow. The prickly hair of his chest rubs against mine with each breath, sending a reminder of how close our bodies remain.

"Was it enough, Alexa, or enough for now?"

"I'm not sure I'll ever get enough of you." I bury my face into the crook of his neck. We lie together, covered only in our sweat.

"You realize that this changes everything, right? You have to get your stuff and bring it over here."

"Are you asking me, or telling me?" I feel him stiffen a bit. I'm not sure he's used to anyone questioning him.

"Which approach will get me what I want?" His fingers glide up and down my arm. He has such a light touch for a big man.

"I've spent most of my life getting bossed around by people. I'd like to be asked for once."

He raises his body and balances his weight on his elbow. My head slides to the pillow beside him. His free hand brushes my cheek sweetly. He doesn't speak at first. It's like he's measuring his words carefully.

"Alexa, you are a surprise. I didn't expect to find you

on the side of the road. I've learned lately that sometimes it's the surprises that mean the most. Look at Aaron, one day I was a single bar owner, and the next day I'm a father. He's one of the best things to have happened to me." He looks past me as if recalling a distant memory. "Something tells me that you're the next best thing in my life. I know it seems quick, and I know that your life has been difficult. I'm asking you to move in with me, and give us a chance."

I look at him and know without a doubt that he understands who I am. He gets me, he sees me. His actions never reduce me, but always empower and uplift me. The choice is mine, and I choose him.

"I'm totally in love with the fact that you asked. Yes, I'll move in. I want to contribute by paying rent or helping with Aaron."

His lips crush into mine. His body lays half off and half on me.

"I'm happy to have you contribute by helping with Aaron, but there is no rent. I own the bar and the house. What I want from you is your friendship and eventually your love."

Wow, he's laying it all on the line right here. It's hard to say no to him. I already know that I could fall in love with him, if I let myself. Maybe it's time I let myself.

"You can have everything I have to give." I'm a bit damaged from my ex, but it's time to move forward. I need to learn to trust again and not hold every man responsible for the sins of one.

"Right now, all I want is your sexy body connected with mine. Are you game or are we done for the day?"

"It's such a chore to have you pleasure me endlessly, but I'm willing to make the sacrifice." I try to say it with a straight face, but I end up in a fit of giggles.

He stops my laugh with a passionate kiss. For the next twenty minutes, we dance between the sheets. I try to give more than I take this time, but taking what Zane has to offer is easy.

He looks at the clock as I look at the ceiling.

"We have just enough time to shower before the little guy begins to stir." He rolls out of bed and walks to the bathroom. This is the first time that I've seen him fully nude. His butt is a solid mass of muscle. Each cheek flexes with every step. "Are you joining me?"

"Nope, I'm going to make coffee and start breakfast. I'm afraid if I get in the shower with you, I'll get distracted, and we'll just get dirty again."

"I can't argue with you there. With you around, I'm pretty positive that I'm going to be distracted frequently."

He walks into the bathroom; I hear the shower start and his voice calls out above it. "Coffee is in the cabinet to the right side of the sink."

I slide out of bed and search for my T-shirt. I have no idea where it went once it was stripped off me. I take his discarded shirt from the dresser and slide it over my head. It smells like him.

I peek in on Aaron before I work my way to the kitchen. I watch his lips pucker while he sleeps. His legs are tucked underneath him with his little behind pushed in the air. I leave him to his slumber, while I go to care for his daddy.

The coffee is just where he said it was. Once I get it brewing, I check the refrigerator for breakfast items. It looks like cheese omelets and toast. Shopping is a must-do chore after I move my things over. He's missing the staples this girl needs.

"Wow, I didn't expect you to cook for me, but I have to say it smells great." He takes two cups out of the cupboard and pours us coffee. He stands behind me and spreads kisses down the side of my neck. I could get used to this.

Just as I plate up our breakfast, I hear the wail of a hungry baby. Zane begins to rise from his seat to get his boy.

"Can I get him? I've been dying to hold him. I'll grab him and change him, and you can get his bottle ready."

"Knock yourself out. I'll cover your omelet, so it doesn't get cold."

"Thanks." I plant a quick kiss on his lips and go to rescue a very unhappy camper.

"Hey, little man. What's wrong? Are you wet? Let's get you changed." I pick up the baby and walk him to the changing table. "Guess what? I get to see you more often. Your dad and I are trying to get to know each other better. I hope that's okay?" I unzip his pajamas and remove his wet diaper. Not wanting to be drenched by his perfect aim I lay a receiving blanket across his waist. "I fell for you the minute I saw you. Your dad took an extra day to wind himself around my heart. I was doomed the minute I met you both." I promptly slide the diaper under his tiny bottom and fasten the Velcro tabs. "Listen, little man, your daddy is an amazing person, and I will be so happy if you grow up to be just like him." I finish my one sided conversation while dressing him, and pull him to my chest for a hug and a kiss.

We emerge from the hallway and find Zane sitting at the table, beaming.

"What are you smiling at?" I cradle the baby in my arms and begin to feed him his morning bottle.

"The baby monitor was on. I'm glad you like us both, and you want him to grow up just like me. That might be the biggest compliment ever paid to a man."

I look around the kitchen and see the monitor as plain as day sitting on the counter. I'm so embarrassed that my private moment with Aaron was broadcast for Zane to hear.

"I'm so embarrassed. We were bonding, and you heard it all."

"It was lovely to hear." He uncovers my plate and takes the baby from me so that I can eat.

"You shouldn't be eavesdropping. Aaron and I were having a secret conversation about you. Well, I was talking, and he was listening." I put a forkful of egg and cheese into my mouth so I can't say anymore.

"You don't have to be embarrassed, I'm totally happy that I've wound my way into your heart. I wanted to be there before I wound my way into your pants. Things are working out perfectly." He smiles at me.

"Yes, I'm thinking you two are in cahoots with one another to win my heart."

"What do I have to do to get what I want?"

I laugh uncontrollably. The sound pours from me and

lot of sex in my life, but what we had today was epic."

Epic? He's trying to make me move in with him and love him all in one day.

"When it comes to hotel sex, I didn't envision our first away experience to be at Shady Lane," I say as his body presses me into the mattress.

"I'll make it up to you. We can go anywhere you want. Where do you want to go, Alexa?"

"I'll have to get back to you on that. Right now I have a hot man that wants to make love to me in a motel."

We spend way too much time in bed. He finally pulls away from me at 11:15 a.m. He's late for work. I'm pretty sure that, as the owner, he's not getting into trouble unless one of his patrons is waiting on him.

"I was supposed to be helping you. Now I have to leave you to pack on your own."

"I like *your* kind of help. Now, go open the bar, and I'll be over in a bit. Can you reserve my table? I have work to do."

"Don't take too long, or I'll have to come looking for you."

"Go away, or I'll never get there." I push him out the door and shut it behind him.

I toss my clothes in my bag and pack up my

toiletries. I look around and see my little pile of fast food by the microwave. Two cans of Beanie Weenies and a can of beef stew remain. I consider throwing it in my bag, but hear Zane's voice telling me to not eat that canned crap and decide to leave it behind.

I walk to the door for the last time. Looking over my shoulder, I say goodbye to my safe haven. I take the key to Trudy, who gives me a sly smile. She may be old, but she has eyes and ears.

"Take care of that sexy man, he needs a strong woman in his life. He's a good man."

"I will, Trudy. Come and see me across the street, okay?"

"Sure thing, darlin'." I give her a quick hug and hop into my pile of junk car to drive across the street.

It's a short move, but one that's not driven by fear. My personal compass drives me, and it's pointing straight toward Zane. This could be another mistake, but deep in my core it's the only choice for me to make. I'm taking a leap of faith and it's resting on the shoulders of an amazing man with his adorable boy.

Chapter Twelve

It doesn't take long to carry my stuff upstairs. I only have one suitcase and some personal hygiene items.

Ashley glares at me when I walk in without knocking. I'm sure that she feels I'm a usurper.

"Zane tells me that you and Claire are the best sitters available in Sugar Glen. He's so lucky to have you."

She looks up at me and smiles. It has to be tough on her to have things change so swiftly.

"I've been here for as long as Aaron has been living here. He's like family to me."

"Well, I'm not planning to replace you if you think my presence is in any way threatening. Both of the men in this house have wrapped themselves around my heart, too."

She seems to relax a bit. She surprises me with her next statement.

"Mr. Abbamonte seems happier since you've been around. He smiles more, and he's not as grumpy."

"Good, I'm glad I'm making a difference. Anyway, I'm heading to Walmart for food and stuff. Do you need anything?"

"Yes, some kind of junk food. This house never has any good snacks." She rolls her eyes skyward. I totally understand. A girl needs junk to survive.

"I have a thing for Nutty Bars, so there will always be some on hand. Make sure to help yourself."

I pick up my purse and take the front stairs down to tell Zane where I'm going.

"Do you need anything specific from the store? I'm heading out to do some shopping."

"Yes, we probably need more condoms," he whispers in my ear. "If we are going to use three or four a day, then I'm pretty certain we'll run out soon."

I pull him around the corner so I can speak to him privately.

"I don't think I could sustain three or four times a day. I'm already walking a bit gingerly, and it's my first day back in the saddle."

"Are you cutting me off already? I didn't think that happened until much further down the road in our relationship."

"I'm not cutting you off, I may be limiting your rides. I have to be able to walk if I'm going to wait tables."

"If waiting tables or having amazing sex with you are

my two choices, then you're fired, I'll take option two."

"You're impossible." I stretch to kiss him.

"I am, but you still love me." He quirks his eyebrow up as if he's trying to challenge me to deny his statement.

"I would say I'm in "deep like" at this point. Love and trust are open for grabs." I wink at him so he doesn't feel disheartened. He chuckles. "Now, back to the list. Do we need diapers?"

"No, I picked up some the other day. I drive to West Cliff every other Friday to pick up bulk items. I was returning from there when I found you."

"Really? So, will you go next Friday? Can I go?"

"Yes and yes. Tomorrow is my mom's time with the baby. Will you come with us?"

"Of course, do you think I'm letting those women at the complex fawn all over my men? Fat chance."

"You look sexy when you're jealous. I like it." His lips broaden slowly into a gorgeous, warm smile. I know what those lips can do, so I start to feel tingly all over. When this man smiles, he should come with a warning label: Back Away.

"Well, it's not an emotion I'm used to. I don't know how to wear it yet. As for the condoms, are you using them so you don't get me pregnant, or are you concerned with getting something from me, considering the lifestyle of my ex-husband?" How will I respond if he thinks I'm a sexual risk? I can't really blame him. Honestly, I would wear a condom if I knew his last partner was involved in risky behavior. She was just stupid and irresponsible. I've been there, and I paid the ultimate price for my stupidity.

He pulls me tightly against his chest and squeezes the air from my lungs. His hand strokes my back. The breath I take is filled with his scent. He always smells so fresh and clean. It's relaxing to be held in his arms.

"Listen to me. I'm not worried about getting anything from you. You've told me that you've been tested many times. I trust you. I'm just not ready to have two babies in diapers." He gently pushes me away from him, and grimaces.

The breath I am unconsciously holding seeps through my lips. It's an amazing feeling to know that he isn't afraid of me. I was afraid for myself for the longest time.

"I'm on the pill. There was no use stopping it just because I wasn't sexually active. If you feel safer wearing condoms, I'm happy to buy them. However, I am diligent about taking my pill."

"Oh, sweets, you just made me the happiest man on earth. I can't wait to feel you. I mean actually feel you against me. Are you sure you want to start limiting my access to your body today? We just started."

"How can I deny you when you make me feel so good?"

"I want to close the bar for the day and go back to Shady Lane to spend the day in bed. This new tidbit of information sends primal urges through my body."

"I'm leaving right now. I need to get a supply of junk food for the girls and me. I can't believe you don't keep a supply of chocolate on hand for Claire and Ashley. You're a horrible boss."

"Candy is awful for you. If you take care of your body, it will take care of you."

"How about you take care of my body, and I'll do what makes me happy?"

"Deal." He slips his hands around me and spins us in a circle. "Drive safely. Do you want to take the car or the truck? I'm not sure I trust that tin jalopy you drive."

"It got me across the street," I tease. "If I have a problem, I'll call you on my phone, and you can send out a rescue squad."

"All right," he says as he reaches for his wallet. "Take some cash for whatever you need."

"Stop it, I'm buying stuff for the house. I want to

pick up a few things to get us through for a few days and also stuff to junk out on. It's my way of contributing."

It takes me about ten minutes to get to the store and about thirty minutes to get everything I need. I was even able to find a baby sling in the infant department. They had more than a few patterns to choose from, so I picked a lovely floral with reds, oranges and yellows.

I can already tell that unloading the groceries is going to be Zane's job. After two trips to the car, there is no doubt in my mind that these stairs are not my friend.

Ashley jumps for joy when she sees the cookies and candy I bought. I'm hoping my small contribution to her comfort helps soften her reticence to my being here.

I put everything away and skip downstairs to work on my project. When I walk through the door into the bar, I can feel the tension in the air.

I look around the room for Zane and find him sitting at a table in the corner by where I usually have my computer set up. I glance around the room to make sure everyone has what they need.

I can only see the back of the woman he is speaking to. She has long, silver-blonde hair. Her bare arms are tattooed from her shoulders to her wrists. She wears blue jeans and a leather vest over what appears to be a red T-shirt. I can see the fabric stretching over her butt.

I catch Zane's eyes as I walk toward my table. He looks uncomfortable. Who's the woman causing him so much trouble? What's her business with my man?

I slide onto a stool and open my computer. I can't hear their conversation clearly, but I pick up the heated parts.

I tune into words like baby and birth. I can't stand to sit here and not know what is going on, so I get up and walk to the bar.

I begin to wipe down every surface, trying to stay occupied. I dart into the kitchen to chat with Bud.

"Hey, Lexi," he says. "I didn't think you came on until four." He's busy using the scraper to clean off the grill. "Can I get you something to eat?"

"I'm good for now. I'm actually just hiding out. I don't want to hang upstairs because I don't want Ashley to feel like I'm watching her, and Zane is having what looks like a private conversation with a woman."

"He tells me that you two are shackin' up." He grins at me, and I see that he's missing a tooth on his lower right.

"Did he actually tell you we were 'shackin' up?'" I finger quote the word shackin'.

"Nah, he said that he convinced you to move upstairs

with him. I'm glad; he's got it bad for you. So, no matter who that woman is, don't get your panties in a twist. He likes you."

Bud is a straight shooter, and I really appreciate his words of encouragement. He delivers them with his own zeal, but I know he's just trying to ease my worry.

I walk back out to the bar and see Zane pouring a beer from the tap.

"I can get that. It looks like you're in a deep conversation." I pull the glass from his hand and seamlessly finish the pour. He gives me a quick kiss before he walks back to the beautiful blonde at the table. I look over at the woman he's talking to. She stares at me with something akin to curiosity. I don't know her, but I don't like her. I don't like her look, and I certainly don't like the way she is getting Zane riled up.

Trying to keep distracted, I pull my phone out of my pocket and dial my sister. It's been a long time since we have spoken. We occasionally email, but that's about it. We used to be really close, but the conflict within my family has made me guarded when it comes to them.

The phone rings three times before her bubbly voice answers with a hello.

"Hi, Ava. It's Alexa." I wait for a glimmer of voice

recognition.

"Oh my God, where are you? Did you finally get to where you're going?" She rattles off a few more questions before I get a word in edgeways.

"I'm good. Actually, I'm better than good. I'm working a lot. One job is doing contract work, and the other is waiting tables at a bar called Last Resort." I glance over at Zane and see that his face is red with fury. "I have a thing going with the owner. It's a really healthy situation for me. It wouldn't be for everyone, but it's been good for me. He has a beautiful little boy named Aaron."

"What? Wait? You're waiting tables? Where are you living? I want to come and see you."

"I'm in Sugar Glen. It's just a few hours outside of Los Angeles. I didn't get very far."

"It sounds like an awful place. Is it even on a map?" I think about that for a few minutes, but I can't honestly answer her. I figure if it exists, it's probably on a map.

"It's a small town, but big enough for a Walmart. The people are really nice, and I finally feel like myself again."

My attention is driven to the table in the corner. I watch in astonishment as the woman pushes away from the table and upends everything on it. She pushes Zane roughly, shoving him into the wall.

"Ava, I gotta go." I hang up abruptly and walk toward the fighting couple. I don't know why I just thought of them as a couple. I suppose it's because they seem like they are familiar with one another. I don't like where my mind is going with this situation.

I get about five feet from them when I hear something that punches me right in the gut.

"I came in here thinking I could see my baby and you tell me no. Who do you think you are?" Her eyes turn to me as she spews out the rest of her venom. "I find you looking like a lovesick puppy. What is she to you? She isn't even your type. She looks like a fucking schoolteacher. You and I both know that you'll fuck her and forget her. You're not the settling down type."

"You don't know me, Tabitha. I fucked you once and forgot about you, but that's not my MO, and even if it were, you changed that by abandoning my baby at a hospital in San Francisco. You have no right to see him." The woman begins to cackle. I don't know what she finds so funny. Zane's eyes look toward me and then back at the woman standing in front of him. "You are the worst kind of person. The only credit I'll give you is that you didn't abort him. That would have been unforgivable."

His words rip at my heart. I start forward again, but

I'm stopped with her final declaration.

"You're so gullible, Zane. The baby you picked up isn't even yours. You were the only number I had, and I wanted someone to pay my bill." She turns around, leaving him standing there with his mouth open.

She walks straight toward me. I stumble back a few steps; not trusting what she intends to do. As soon as she is in front of me, she pushes on my shoulder and begins screaming at me.

"You're stupid if you think he wants you. He's a biker. He's using you to take care of that baby he has. I can't believe how stupid people can be."

Rage overtakes me. I have been pushed around so much in my life. I have allowed the people who were supposed to love me, hurt me, but I refuse to let this stranger do it.

Feeling like I'm having an out-of-body experience, I reach up grab a handful of her hair. I begin walking her—dragging her—to the door. When we get within a few feet of the entrance, I tug extra hard and come away with a handful of blonde hair.

"Get out of this bar, and don't ever fucking come back. You gave them both up, and now it's time for you to move on."

I toss her on her ass outside the door and go about my business. When I look up, I see the smiles of several patrons and the shocked look in Zane's face.

He walks into the kitchen and comes back with Bud. His fingers intertwine with mine.

"Let's go." He pulls me through the kitchen and out the back door. We sit on the picnic bench and embrace the silence of the moment.

Will he be angry with me for kicking that woman out on her ass? It wasn't my place, but I couldn't stand there and watch her create more havoc. She had just finished telling this wonderful man that the boy he's raising isn't his.

"Alexa, I want you to know that you are not in my life because I need a babysitter. I have plenty of volunteers for that."

I think back to our visit at his mom's house, and I'm sure all he would need to do is smile, and nearly every woman in town would be here in a heartbeat.

I hear the distant ringing of a phone, but I can't place where it's coming from. He reaches behind me and grabs the phone from my pocket.

I shake my head feeling a bit stupid that I didn't even recognize my own ringtone. I flip it open and say hello.

"Yes, I'm okay." I say in between her frantic questions. "No, it's not a dangerous place. Listen, I have to go. I'll call you later." I hang up the phone and place it on the bench.

"Who is that?" he asks. His hand reaches over and takes mine. The warmth of his touch runs up my arm and down my back. Every nerve in my body seems to be on alert. It must be the adrenaline coursing through me that has ignited my desire.

I'm incredibly sore between my legs, but if he asked me to have sex right here on the table, I fear I would surrender without an argument.

"It's my sister. I called her as a distraction in the bar."

"Alexa, look at me." He pinches my chin between his thumb and index finger and raises my face to look into his. I stare into his eyes. There is a range of emotions surfacing, but the one I see the clearest is concern. "You're here because we connect on some level that's special. I'm not a love them and leave them guy. That's not my motto, and I don't want you to think that it is."

"I didn't think that. Are you really worried about that? I see you for who you are. I know you're a good man." I cup the side of his cheek and feel him relax. "That

184

woman tells you that Aaron is not yours, and your first concern is whether or not I think that you're using me?"

"Oh God, this is so awful," he says. He buries his head in his hands and groans.

"Aaron only knows you. You are the only father he's had. I'm sorry that she hurt you by her claim. I'm not sure that she would even know the truth." I run my fingers through his hair. "He's lucky to have you. I hope that you can see past this and not punish him for her sins."

"It doesn't matter to me whose sperm created that boy. The day I held him, he became mine. I may not be his biological father, but I'm damn sure I'm his dad."

Chapter Thirteen

His truth hits me like a sledgehammer to the head. Here is this man who has just found out his son possibly has no genetic connection to him, and he's worried I may feel offended by the twat-head of a woman who birthed Aaron.

I feel my emotions surging out of control. I know where this is going, and I need to escape quickly. Every hurt I've ever felt is coming to the surface. I'm going to an ugly place. There is no stopping it.

He sees the change in my demeanor. I can tell by the way he grabs me and pulls me to his chest. I struggle against him as I try to get away. I need to run. I need to hide.

I thought I was over this and had maneuvered through the triggers. I was so sure that I had a handle on all of it, but now I know that it is just a lie I told myself to survive.

I push against his chest trying to break his grip on me, but he holds on tighter. He's not letting go. If I don't get away, he'll see everything.

"Let me go," I scream. I tug and pull, but he holds me more firmly.

"I'm not going to let you go. I know that you feel threatened by Tabitha, but she means nothing to me. I'm with you, and there is no place I would rather be."

"You can't mean that, you have no idea what I've been through. Here you are, sitting in the bar, and someone tells you that Aaron is not yours. You don't even blink an eye. In your heart, he's yours," I continue to struggle against him, but I'm no match for his strength. I finally collapse into him and let my sobs unfold. The pain is so sharp that I think my heart is hemorrhaging. I'm positive if someone poked my chest with a needle I would bleed out. My heart is shredding to pieces.

"Alexa, I care about you. In fact, after you tossed Tabitha out on her ass, I'm pretty sure I fell in love with you. What's going on, sweetheart?" His lips brush the top of my head. He shifts his position and pulls me into his lap. I'm trapped in his vise-like grip.

My sobbing is nearing hysteria. I'm pretty sure if I tell him everything, he's going to want me to leave. He told Tabitha that it would have been unforgivable if she had killed their baby. What would he think about me?

His chest raises and lowers against the side of my face. His shirt is soaked in my tears. I wipe my nose on my sleeve and begin to choke on my sorrow.

"Shh, it's okay. Whatever it is, it's going to be all right." He holds me for what seems like a lifetime. So much time has passed that the sun has set, and night is approaching. I feel him move, and before I know it, he is carrying me up the back steps.

When we enter the house, he takes me directly to his room and closes the door with a tap from his foot. Softly my body touches the bed. He pulls my shoes off my feet and lets them hit the ground where he stands. He pulls off my jeans and tucks me under the covers.

"I need to check on Bud, but I'll be right back. Don't go anywhere. I mean it, Alexa. If you disappear on me, I will track you down." He walks to the door and looks back at me.

I bury my face in his pillow and soak the cover with heart wrenching sobs. Time doesn't exist in my world right now. Everything is upside down and backward. It feels like he's been gone a few minutes, but when I glance at the clock, I see that it's been over an hour. I've let him down. I'm supposed to be helping in the bar, and I've left him and Bud short-handed.

I hear voices outside the doorway. I don't want to see anyone right now. I just want to curl up in a ball and disappear. The door creaks open. A stream of light rushes in, nearly blinding me.

"It's me. I'm sorry it took me so long. I had to help Bud with the rush. He sent up some soup and tea. I told him you weren't feeling well."

I lift myself into a sitting position to make room for Zane. He carries the soup-laden tray to the bed and sits it on my lap.

"I'm not really hungry," I say with a voice I hardly recognize. Crying for hours can wreak havoc on your vocal chords.

"You're eating, even if I have to feed you myself." He scoots in next to me and picks up the soupspoon. I watch as he dips it into the broth and lifts it to my mouth. I open just enough to take a bite.

"I can do it," I say as I pull the utensil from his hand. "We've talked about this bossy side of you. It's all right if you want to try it on for size, but I'm not buying it." I'm trying to steer the conversation in a different direction because if we start talking about me; it's not going to go well.

"You can try to deflect the subject all you want, but

we're getting through this tonight. The faster we get it done, the sooner we can fall asleep in each other's arms."

I sip the soup as big crocodile tears roll down my cheeks and fall into the bowl. What if he doesn't want me in his arms after he learns the truth? He picks the tray up and deposits it on the dresser.

Lying next to each other, he looks in my direction and tells me to start from the beginning.

I feel my panic begin to rise. Bile billows up from my stomach and burns my throat. I say a silent prayer for God to get me through this night. Tomorrow will be a new day. Tomorrow I'll venture forward to a new town, a new life.

I take a deep breath before I begin.

"My baby was aborted," I blurt out. A silent stream of tears pours from my eyes.

"What are you talking about? What baby? Did you choose to abort your child as opposed to having it? Is that what you're telling me." He looks stunned by the information.

"I'm telling you that I was pregnant toward the end of my marriage. I'm not even sure how it happened. We had sex on Wednesdays, and that's it. I took my pills faithfully. I didn't realize that a bout of strep throat and a series of antibiotics would create a window for conception." I pause a minute trying to get my thoughts straight.

"It was a decision you made, Alexa. I can't be angry with you after hearing what a jackass your ex-husband is. I also can't absolve you of your guilt. I'm not going to judge you for your choice, and, by the way, people do get pregnant on Wednesdays." I smile on the inside at his gracious attempt to console me with humor.

"I heard you tell Tabitha that aborting Aaron would have been unforgivable. Why is my sin any less than hers would have been?"

"It's not, it's just that I know what I would be missing. When a baby smiles at you for the first time, something happens to the way you think about things. I've always been pro-choice. I'm just glad that she didn't abort my son."

The mention of his son tears me apart. I begin blubbering. In my head, I'm making sense, but I'm obviously not saying anything that makes sense to Zane.

"Alexa, you need to stop crying. I can't understand a word you're saying." He takes his thumb and gently wipes the tears from my eyes.

"Tyler killed my child." The sobs continue.

"What the fuck, Alexa? You just said you aborted

your child. What do you mean Tyler killed your child?" I have his attention now. He's no longer sitting next to me; he's pacing the room.

"I didn't abort my child, but I failed to protect him or her. Isn't that the same?" The truth weighs heavily on my heart. The crushing pain from the weight of honesty is squeezing my chest, wringing the will to live from my body.

He rushes to my side and pulls me against him. I rub my face into his chest. I wish I could crawl inside his body. Anywhere but here would be good, and yet, here is exactly where I want to be. With him I can breathe, without him I perish.

"No, it's not the same. What did that fucker do to you?"

His anger is palpable. I can feel the energy he's emitting sizzle through the air.

"I found out I was pregnant a few weeks before we separated. It wasn't what broke us up. He had already worked everything out. He worked his way into becoming a partner in my dad's business. He had stayed the required amount of time to walk away a wealthy man." I move so that I can look at him as I speak. I need to see his eyes. "I threw a wrench in the works. I got pregnant. I was thrilled about having a baby. Finally, Tyler was giving me something I wanted. He hadn't given me anything else in our marriage, but he did give me a child."

"What happened?" he asks. I can tell he's anxious to get to the bottom of this.

"When I told him I was pregnant, he lost his mind. He was furious. He turned over furniture and tore art off the walls as he made his way to the door. I couldn't understand how a man could be so angry. I had just told him he'd created a child, and he threw a fit." I roll off the side of the bed and walk to the dresser to pick up the tea. My throat feels parched and sore. "He disappeared for several days. I was frantic with worry. At that time, I didn't know about his lifestyle choice. I had no idea he had a boyfriend who was waiting for him to leave me. He showed up a few days later and found me in bed. I had cried so many tears that my eyes were swollen almost completely shut, and my head pounded."

I toss back the remainder of the tea and return to my place on the bed.

"When he came home I was relieved. He was so sweet and apologetic. I felt like he had taken the time to think about his child and had come to the realization it was going to be wonderful to parent a little human being. He brought me two Ibuprofen and a glass of water. I thought it was a lovely gesture from a caring husband. I couldn't have been more wrong."

He shifts his position and pulls me between his legs. I can no longer see his face, but he gives me the courage to continue with the way he holds me protectively in his embrace. I feel like he's saying "I've got you."

"I should have known something was off. He slept in our bed that night and the next night. He stayed by my side for two days. On the third day after he had come back, I began to hemorrhage. I panicked. Tyler took me to the hospital and played the concerned, doting husband. I spent the night in the ER. I was told early the next morning I had miscarried."

Strong arms tighten around me. This man is treating me with more compassion than my husband of four years could have mustered in any given moment.

"I went home that afternoon and locked myself in my room for days. I was devastated. Had my child lived, he or she would be almost the same age as Aaron."

"You're kidding me?" It's the first thing he's said since I began my story.

"No, I'm not. That's why I totally freaked out the day you left me with him. There was no way that I wanted the responsibility of another child when I had failed mine so miserably."

"I'm confused. First I thought you aborted your baby, then you said Tyler murdered your child, and now you're saying it was a spontaneous miscarriage. I need clarification."

"I'm getting there," I tell him. "Two weeks after I lost the baby, he asked for a divorce. Well, it was more like he brought the paperwork home and asked me to sign. I was shocked. That's when things got really interesting. He started openly flaunting his love for men. He even brought a man home one night and made love to him in our bed. I asked him how he could be so cruel, especially after I had just lost our child. He told me to shut the fuck up, and that he never wanted me to mention the baby again. He went on a tirade about how stupid I was to think he would ever allow me to have his kid. I found out through one of his outbursts that what I had thought were aspirin for my headache was, in fact, the RU486—the morning after pill. He double-dosed me to make sure that I would lose the baby. So you see, he murdered my child, and then took everything else from me."

He turns me in his lap and looks into my eyes.

"How is any of this your fault? He drugged you. He

lied to you, and he took from you. He stole your spirit, your trust and your self-esteem." His lips press into mine. I didn't expect to end our conversation with a kiss, but I'm relieved he didn't turn around and run.

"I should have known better. I heard the warnings throughout my entire marriage. I told my parents something was wrong, but he'd hypnotized them with his charm and cunning. He stole from my whole family. He stole my family. In the end, he took their livelihood, and they blamed me for marrying him."

"Isn't that rich? They basically pushed you down the aisle and when everything went to shit they blamed you. I don't think I like your parents."

"I don't like them either, but on some level I can't fault them. I was caught up in his charm as well."

"You said you had a civil suit against him. What was that about?"

"I tried to charge him with physical and mental abuse. Unfortunately, there was no drug testing done when I lost the baby. I couldn't prove he'd actually drugged me, even though he openly admitted it to me. In the end, he got away with murder. It was my word against his."

"I want to kill him. I can't believe he got away with all of that. Is he's still in Los Angeles?"

"Yes, he lives with his pharmacy tech boyfriend in our old house. I left everything. I didn't have the energy to fight. He had worked everything out so it would fall in his favor. I left with my purse and what cash I had in my bank account. I bought what I needed along the way."

"I'm so sorry. You're an amazingly strong woman. I'm so impressed with you. Aaron and I are lucky men to have you in our lives." He shifts us both so he can get up. "I'm going to run a bath for you. While you relax, I'm going to close up the bar and send Ashley home. She is worried about you."

"I'm okay. There won't be another outburst. Everything was triggered when you said you didn't care whether Aaron was yours or not. All I could think was that my ex-husband killed his own child, and you've done everything to save someone else's."

Zane kisses me slowly. He draws me a bath and leaves me to my thoughts. I reflect on the evening and how he'd held me and cared for me. He supported me and didn't pass judgment. If I didn't love him before, I love him now, but do I deserve him? Once again, he's freed me from something; tonight it's guilt. I've been carrying around the heavy weight of this burden in my heart and he's erased it with his compassion and love. Is it possible that he loves me?

Chapter Fourteen

I wake up with a squirming ball of energy, flapping his arms next to me. Zane is lying on his side looking at his son and me. His eyes are soft and relaxed.

"Good morning, beautiful. We thought we would see if you wanted to get up and see grandma with us." He leans over Aaron and plants a quick kiss on my lips.

"Of course, isn't it breakfast sandwich day? There's no way I'm missing that. I also bought your mom a gift and I want to give it to her."

"A gift? What did you get her?" He reaches down and plays with the baby's feet. They look so small compared to his hands.

"I bought a baby sling, and I thought we could give it to her together."

He looks at me and then looks at the baby between us.

"Aaron...look at how lucky we are," he says. "We have a smart, sexy and generous woman looking out for us."

I lie on my back and look up at the ceiling. It seems like yesterday was a lifetime ago.

He picks the baby up and settles him on his chest. We are now both lying on our backs looking at the ceiling.

"Are you doing okay this morning? I worried about you all night. I was frightened I would wake up and you would be gone. I was afraid to open my eyes."

"I had every intention of leaving. I thought after you knew the truth; you would want me to go, but you responded differently than I expected you to." My hand finds his on the bed next to me. I lace my fingers through his.

"I'm doing a poor job of convincing you I'm a good guy. What can I do to make you realize that I am totally into you?"

"It's not you. I'm conditioned not to trust. I'm working through it. What you did for me last night was incredible. You held me for hours; you listened to me, you heard me. I know that you're an amazing man, I'm just not sure if I'll be enough for you."

"I'm crazy for you. I can't get enough of you. I'm praying Aaron falls asleep so I can put him down, and I can make love to you." I see that his bundle of energy has slipped into a peaceful nap. He may just get his wish. "I want you to feel my love, Alexa." His beautiful lips start to form his irresistible, alpha-man smile. *Now I'm in trouble.* He places his hands carefully over Aaron's tiny ears and whispers, "Actually, I think I need to pound it into you so you'll be completely convinced."

As I smile at his naughty but delicious comment, a single tear slips from the corner of my eye. He basically just told me that he wanted to screw me hard, but there was something in there that said I'm here for the long haul, and I want you with me. I stand up and gently lift the sleeping form off of his chest.

"Looks like you got your wish. Let me put him down so we can get lost in one another for a few minutes, and then we have to head off to your mom's."

He lies naked on the bed. His body is like a finely chiseled sculpture. Everything about him is beautiful, from his broad shoulders to his crooked little toes. I pull off my T-shirt; it's the only thing I'm wearing besides my underwear.

I crawl next to him and snuggle into his side. He rolls away from me and straddles my body. His fingers slip beneath my underwear and shimmy them down. I am completely exposed to him. He's seen my body before, but now he sees everything. He's gotten a glimpse of my deepest darkest parts, and he still wants me. I no longer feel vulnerable, but feel strengthened. Precious.

He nips and kisses every inch of my body. My head rolls back in bliss as he settles his lips in my most intimate area. His warm mouth draws out every moan as my hips dance to his rhythm. He takes me to the edge and holds me there until I'm begging for release. He sucks on my flesh, sending me into a turbulent explosion of sensation. I ride the waves of my release until I feel the weight of the mattress shift.

"I want to make love to you. Just you and me and nothing in between. Are you okay with that?"

Breathless and speechless, I nod my head to consent. He climbs between my legs and hovers over my body. Although we have a limited amount of time, he takes things slowly, starting with a long lingering kiss.

His lips tease mine before he captures my mouth with hungry urgency. He devours me like a starving man would eat a meal. The softness of his tongue tangles with mine.

Slowly he enters me. My heart lurches as he fills me completely. We move together simultaneously, our hips rocking to some primal beat. I hold his arms as he rocks me with his love.

Isn't it ironic I can meet a man who gives everything,

shortly after leaving a man who took so much away?

His pace slows as our eyes connect. It feels like he's looking into my soul. He utters three words before he spills himself deep inside of me. He collapses on top of me breathless and sweaty. I stroke his back as I think of those three words, "We belong together."

My heart skips a beat at his words. As much as I want to say them in return, I can't. To verbalize what's in my heart is too risky. Will he continue to want me, and if he doesn't, will I survive?

After lying together for a while enjoying the quiet moment, we reluctantly leave the bed. We shower, then race around the room trying to get ready to leave. While I brush my hair and put on a dab of makeup, he gets the little man ready for our visit.

We swing by the diner to pick up the egg sandwiches that Zane has ordered. I run in to get them, and we are on our way.

Miraculously, we're only ten minutes late. He unhooks the car seat while I pick up breakfast, the baby bag and our gift to his mother.

We make it through the lobby fast. The women part like a scattered flock before a lion as soon as we tell them that we're late.

Today, Elaine is waiting with the door open. She smiles broadly as we approach. She reaches for me first and hugs me with her shaking body.

Zane smiles at me. Actually, he's grinning from ear to ear. I imagine it's a good morning for him. Most men would love to start their morning off with sex followed by food. But with Zane, there is also the genuine happiness to see his Mom.

"What are you grinning at?" I walk past him and into the apartment. I drop Aaron's bag by the sofa and bring the food to the table. I look over my shoulder and see mother and son ogling the baby.

I remember hearing someone once tell me that the best way to know how a man will treat you is to watch him with his mother. The love he has for his mother is evident in everything that he does. He's a keeper.

Elaine loves the sling. While she sits feeding the baby, Zane takes me for a walk around the complex. I think it was more for his mom than for us. Having us sit and watch her with the baby must be what it feels like to have supervised visits with your child.

"Today is probably the best day of my life," he says as he pushes me gently against the wall. I am trapped between the siding and his body. "It's more than the sex.

You need to understand that." His eyes capture mine, and I see the sincerity with which he speaks. "I know this is crazy; it shouldn't be possible, but I love you. You trusted me last night. You stayed and let me take care of you. I need that from my partner. You complete me, Alexa." He sees everything I am, and everything I will be, and he isn't running.

"I do need you, and I feel you complete me, too. I didn't realize how much I needed to be nurtured and cared for until last night. I don't want to love you, but I do. I don't want to need you, but I can't help myself. I feel your love, and I never want to know what it's like to live without it." Those are the most honest words I've told anyone in a long time. It's scary to expose your heart, but he makes it easy.

"I'm happy to hear it. Fate brought us together for whatever reason and I'm not going to question it." We stare at each other in silence before he breaks the spell. "Do you think it's time to rescue our boy?" *Our* boy. Wow. Loving that. His eyes travel down to my lips before he begins a sweet invasion of my mouth. I return his kiss with equal zeal. We reluctantly pull away from each other.

"It's probably time to rescue your mother," I say as I pull my fingers to my lips. Every kiss with him leaves me wanting more. We walk back to her home, hand in hand.

Friday and Saturday are busy at the bar. We fall into bed exhausted each night. By closing time Sunday, all we want is delivery pizza, the couch, and each other.

The baby is fast asleep on my chest, and it feels so right. When I dream of a family, this is my vision.

"Don't forget that we have a date tomorrow night." His hand covers my knee and squeezes it gently.

"Do you realize that this is our first date? Look at us. We have a baby, and we've never had dinner out," I say.

"We're definitely non-conventional, but I think it works."

"I don't really want to leave him with anyone. Should we take him with us?"

"Sweets, he'll be fine. We need time away from the bar and away from the baby."

I know he's right. However, I'm not willing to give up anything right now. Selfish as it may seem, I want it all, and I want it now. I'm a modern day Veruca Salt.

"What are we going to do?" I'm curious as to what our first date is going to look like.

"I thought we would have dinner and see a movie. Then I'm going to bring you home, and make love to you all night."

"Ooh, that sounds wonderful. We could skip dinner, and the movie, and just go for option three."

"Wow, look at you. Wednesday you were thinking of withholding and today your throttle is fully engaged. Why the change?"

"Just for the record, I wasn't considering withholding because I didn't want to have sex, I was thinking about withholding because I wanted to be able to walk. When you unleash that thing, it delivers quite a wallop."

The roar of his laughter sends me into hysterics. Poor Aaron is awakened from a sound sleep. His little arms flail about until he calms himself and falls back to sleep on my chest.

"Why don't you put him down for the night and I'll meet you in our bed." He gives me a wink and a seductive smile as he walks into our room. It's funny to think of it as ours. One of the things I love about Zane is he is very giving. He's opened his life and home to me. He's given me full access to his child and his heart.

"I can't believe how easily he falls back to sleep," I say to Zane as I enter the bedroom. He lies naked on the bed. His chest is exposed, but a white sheet drapes over his lower body like a beautifully wrapped package.

"Come to bed and hurry. Who knows when he'll wake up? This baby thing puts a damper on romance."

"Yes, it does, but it increases your ability to be spontaneous. I also think it makes us think about sex more often. Don't you find yourself thinking about his next nap?" I can't believe I'm having this conversation with him. It's a wonderful feeling to know that I'm free to be me.

People who say they spend hours making love are obviously childless. You can push all the buttons in less time and still enjoy the act. When you know that you're going to be up with a baby in a few hours, sleep takes on a much more significant role. At this point, I'm going with the adage that quality is better than quantity.

Chapter Fifteen

I'm beginning to love Mondays. They are usually the bane of existence for the average person, but for Zane and me, they are the one day that we have free from responsibility. Sure, we have a baby, but the bar is closed, and we don't have anywhere to be.

I crawl out of the big bed in search of the man who rocked my world last night. I pull his big T-shirt over my head and let it fall to my knees. I find him in the kitchen with a baby in one hand and a phone in the other. His back is turned to me.

"Yes, that's right. It's important justice is served. I'm going to try to be there. Things are complicated."

I reach around him and place a kiss on his back. I sneak around the front and smile at Aaron. Taking him from his dad's arms, I lift him over my head and make faces at him. He breaks into a smile. It's the first one I've ever squeezed out of him. I'm overjoyed he recognizes me or at least thinks I have a funny face.

With the baby in my arms, I set about making coffee.

I hear Zane finishing up his conversation. He comes up behind me and presses his body against mine.

"Did you sleep well?" His lips tickle my skin from the base of my ear all the way to my shoulder. His shirt has fallen off one of my shoulders giving him unfettered access.

"Mmm hmm," I murmur as I lean back into his body. "Do you want some coffee?"

"Yes, I do, and then I was thinking about a run, seeing as how you have distracted me from my fitness regimen all week."

"I haven't distracted you, I've just changed it up. It's important to get a full-body workout. I hear that variety will keep you committed to your plan. You know, they say that it only takes three months to make a habit of something."

"You're already a habit I can't give up. Do you want to join us? I'll buy you breakfast."

"No, I have some shopping to do. I have a hot date tonight, and I want to look extra pretty."

"Is that right? Well, you could show up in sweats and a T-shirt, and your date will be impressed with your beauty, but if you're dating me, I will have to question your good sense."

"Hmm, is there something I should know about you that you haven't shared?"

"Nope, I'm pretty much an open book. A few of my pages are ripped and torn, some are stained, but the content is all there."

"I'm looking forward to turning your pages, Mr. Abbamonte. You never know what you're going to find when you flip to the middle. Ooh, and then there's the end. Will it be a satisfying read?"

"You'll never get to the end of my story, sweets. I'm a work in progress; I'm regularly getting edited and re-released."

"I'm a series. Just when you think the last chapter has been written, another book is released. You know…you're my favorite character so far."

"I'm your only character," he tells me. He pulls the baby from my arms and gives me a kiss. Within thirty minutes my favorite men are gone, and I'm left on my own.

I sip my coffee and look around the house. I remember the first time I saw it. I thought it was warm and masculine. Now as I look through the clouded eyes of a girl in love, it's a perfect place for an imperfect man. The only difference now is that I know his imperfections are small compared to his assets.

My day is spent shopping for the ideal dress. I think that a sundress would work for anything he has in mind tonight. I'm sure we're staying local so we remain close to the baby.

Sugar Glen is a small, but quaint town. It reminds me of something out of a television show. It's a mix between *Mayberry RFD* and *Leave It to Beaver* with a bit of *Gossip Girl* thrown in.

I decide to spend my afternoon on Main Street. If I don't find what I need here, I'll visit my beloved superstore at the edge of town. Daisy's is the first place I visit. It's a boutique that sits in the center of town. The window display is what catches my eye. Mannequins in cute summer dresses and shorts are displayed amidst beach balls and sun umbrellas. It looks happy, and I'm all about the happy these days.

"Can I help you?" the sales associate asks. "You're Alexa, right?"

Surprised this stranger would know my name I stop and give her my undivided attention.

"Hi, how do you know me? I don't think we've ever

met." I cock my head to the side in question. She's pretty, maybe twenty-five, with blonde hair and blue eyes. I'm guessing her name could be Daisy, although I think Melissa is a better fit.

"Everyone knows you. It's a small town. You can't drag a bitch by the hair out of the bar, and not have people talk."

"Oh my God, does everyone know?" I look around me to see who's watching, but it's just her and me.

"Pretty much. You would have to be deaf to have not heard the buzz around town that day. Don't worry though, no one liked her. She thought she was a gift to mankind."

"She was out of line, and she was disrespectful to Zane." I begin to walk around the store while she continues to speak.

"I hear that you and Zane are an item. You moved in with him, right?"

"Wow, nothing gets past you, does it?" I don't know if I should be flattered or flustered.

"Ashley is my baby sister. She told me you moved in and you were sick. I hope you're feeling better." Her smile and concern seem genuine.

"Now that you mention it, you and your sister have similar looks. She's a very sweet girl, and she takes exceptional care of Aaron."

"She loves her job. Zane pays the girls really well, and my sister knows there's a line of women waiting to help out if needed. Although, I'm sure it's dwindling now he's declared you as his."

"This is just a guess, but does your mom work at the assisted living center?" That's the only place he's declared anything in public that I can remember.

"No, my aunt does." She begins to laugh. "What brings you in?"

"I have a date tonight and I wanted to get a new dress. I was drawn in by your window display."

"Well, welcome to Daisy's. I'm Daisy by the way." She reaches out and shakes my hand. "What about this soft blue dress, it's my favorite. When I saw it, I had to buy it. She pulls it from the rack and hands it to me."

It's a cute dress. I like the V-neck, the cinched waist and above-the-knee length. I take it to the dressing room and slip it on. Daisy gave me the perfect size.

"What do you think?" I ask as I walk out of the changing room. I twirl around in front of her.

"I love it. What are you going to do with your hair?" she asks. She reaches up to touch my limp brown locks. "I think you should leave it down with loose curls. You know men. They like long hair."

"That's what I was thinking as well. What about accessories? Can you hook me up?" I can tell I'm speaking her language. She takes my elbow and leads me to a rack near the register. Hanging from the hooks, are cute, one-of-a-kind pieces. I let my fingers skim the glass beads. It's been so long since I felt this happy, this normal.

I rummage through several necklaces to find the yellow creation hanging toward the back.

"What do you think of this one?" I ask as I bring it up to my chest. "I love blue and yellow together."

"I would have picked the same one. I think it's perfect. I have the companion earrings to match if you're interested." She begins to thumb through the rack in search of the ideal earrings.

I change back into my clothes and carry my treasures to the register.

"I appreciate your help today. I hope to see you again. You should come by the bar sometime." I pull out my debit card to make my purchases.

"I think I will. I should hate you for taking the only decent looking bachelor in town, but I can't help but like you. I think you and I are destined to be friends."

"I'd like that, Daisy. Have a great day and make sure

that you stop by and say hi."

She hands me her business card and walks me to the door. This is turning out to be a great day.

When I walk in the house, I am greeted with a vase of fresh flowers on the table. The kitchen is spotless, and the house smells like freshly squeezed lemons.

Zane turns the corner wearing green rubber gloves. In his right hand is a sponge and bottle of cleaner. I have to say, I used to think that a man in a suit was sexy, but a man who cleans is beyond enticing.

"Hey, how was your day out? Did you get what you needed?" He walks up to me and gives me a peck on the lips.

"Yes, it was a phenomenal day. I met a new friend, and I was able to pick up some things I needed. The best part of the day is coming home to find you cleaning. It's the best type of foreplay imaginable. I just love a man with dishpan hands. It's a total turn on."

"Did I mention I do laundry?" he says as he peels off the gloves and pulls me into his arms. "I'm really good with a vacuum as well," he mutters between kisses.

"You're a shameless flirt and just for the record, there's nothing wrong with your suction." I hop up, wrap my legs around his waist, and smother him with my lips.

Judging by his smirk, *and* his erection, I think he liked my reference to his suction.

"The flowers are for my date. Do you think she'll like them?" He places his hands under my bottom and walks me to our room.

"I love them. How did you know I liked mixed flowers?" He drops on the bed and leans over me.

"You are a bit unconventional, so I figured roses are too traditional and carnations are too boring. You're anything but boring, and I think you're turning to the wild side, so a wildflower bouquet seemed appropriate. Before you know it, I'll have you on the back of my bike doing seventy down an open stretch of highway."

"Only seventy? And I thought you were a bad boy?" I bite at his lower lip.

"Ouch," he calls out as he pulls away from me. "I've had to tone my badness down now that I have people depending on me. The only place I can be bad is in the bedroom."

I shake my head back and forth. "I hate to burst your bubble, but when it comes to the bedroom, you're not bad…you're exceptionally good."

Just as he leans in for a kiss our built in romance wrecker lets out a wail that could wake the dead.

"He's becoming less cute with each interruption," he teases.

"I'll get him." I squeeze from beneath Zane and rush to the screaming baby.

I lift him from his crib and pull him to my chest. His crying settles immediately. I take him to the changing table to get him a dry diaper. Once he's changed, we sit in the rocker and have a long talk.

"I got you," I whisper. "I know how scary it is to wake up alone and feel vulnerable. That's how I woke up every day until I met your daddy. We are so lucky to be rescued by him." I kiss his little nose before I stand up to go in search of his next meal.

When I enter the kitchen, my sexy man is leaning against the counter with a prepared bottle in his hand and a grin on his face. His eye travels to the little white box on the counter. He's been eavesdropping again.

"It's not polite to listen in on a private conversation." I try to act as if I'm appalled.

"There are no secrets in this family," he says gruffly. His smile breaks through his stern disposition. He fools no one but himself. "I have to run out for a few minutes, can I leave the baby with you or should I take him with me?"

"Go—we're bonding. I have more secrets to tell him

anyway." I stick my tongue out at him like a child would. I don't know what compelled me to do that, but I did.

"I can think of better things to do with that tongue." He kisses both of us before he opens the back door and disappears.

He's gone about thirty minutes before he trots up the stairs with freshly cut hair.

"Don't you look handsome? Do you have a hot date tonight?" His hair is neatly trimmed, and his face is clean-shaven.

"I do, and my date better put her rear in gear. The sitter is coming in thirty minutes. I want to be gone in forty-five minutes." He takes the baby from my arms, turns me around, and swats my butt.

I emerge forty minutes later, dressed and ready to go. Zane is in the kitchen while Ashley lies on the floor with Aaron.

"You look beautiful," Ashley says.

"Thank you. Your sister helped me pick out my outfit today." I twirl around so she can see the whole picture.

When I come full circle, my eyes look to Zane for some reaction. His eyes sparkle, and his lip twitches before a smile takes over half of his face. He looks pleased with what he sees. We say goodbye to Aaron and Ashley, and step out on our first date.

The restaurant he picked is located on Main Street. It's a small Italian Bistro called Luigi's. We sit at a corner table and sip wine while we share an antipasto salad.

"I know that you didn't like me when you first met me. What changed your mind?" His hand reaches across the table and grabs mine.

"It's not that I didn't like you. You were bossy and verged on the edge of rude. I didn't know you, and you barked orders at me. You told me things I didn't want to hear." His hand completely covers mine. "When I sat back and thought about the things you were most adamant on, I couldn't fault you for your concern. You didn't know me and yet you cared more than those who have known me my whole life."

"I just wanted to see you take care of yourself. I picked up a mess on the side of the road, and in a few days, I watched you relax and show your true colors."

"Do you miss your old life?" I ask.

"Sometimes, I miss certain things. I miss frozen yoghurt and weekend rides up the coast. I miss the coffee shop on the corner and the mall. What do you miss?"

"Honestly, I feel like I fell into a little piece of heaven. This town is full of real people, and I like that. If I had to choose one thing that I miss, it's probably sushi."

"Ah…sushi, I can go for a spicy tuna roll just about now." As soon as he says that, our pasta dishes are delivered.

"Let's play a game. I will toss out a question, and you answer it. It will be like speed dating. We'll bounce things off each other. You go first."

"What's your favorite music?"

He rolls his eyes before he blurts out, "Classic Rock."

"What is your all time favorite movie?" he asks.

"Definitely *Wizard of Oz*. What about you?"

"*Citizen Kane*. What's your favorite candy?"

"Nutty Bars are my ultimate favorite."

"Is that why my cupboard is full of them?"

"Yes. Have you ever had one?"

"No, just the name sounds awful." He makes a face that looks like he tasted something bad.

"What's your favorite pastime, besides having sex with me?" I section my ravioli into bite-size pieces.

"Well, as you know, I love to ride my Harley, but I also love to fly kites."

"Really? I would have never guessed that. Speaking of bikes, I think you should take the weekend ride with your friend next weekend. I promise not to sell your bar or steal your son."

"I've been thinking about that, and I'd like to take you up on your offer, but back to the questions. What's your favorite pastime besides using me for sex?" That little wink of his eye will be my undoing. It's so sexy.

"I like to play pinball, any kind." His eyes dart up in surprise.

"I've never seen you play the games in the bar. Why is that?"

"It's because I'm usually on the clock when I'm in the bar."

"You have my explicit permission to play anytime, whether you are on the clock or not. I'm also willing to give you quarters." I smile at his generosity.

"What's your favorite food?" I thought he would say something like steak, but he surprises me with his answer of tacos, rice and beans.

We banter back and forth through the rest of dinner. It's amazing what you can learn on one date. Every detail he shares makes me love him that much more.

He pays the bill and walks me to the car.

"Are you ready to turn and run, Alexa?"

"Well, you had me until you said that you liked bubble gum ice cream. That's a deal breaker for me. It's mocha almond fudge or nothing."

"All right then, can you find your way home? I need to go in search of a woman who likes bubble gum ice cream."

He watches my mouth drop open and takes advantage with a kiss.

"Do you really want to go to a movie?" I ask. "It's just that, I don't want to spend two hours in a room where I can't touch or talk to you. I would rather go home and spend it in bed."

"Let's compromise. We'll go to the bar, where I will ply you with alcohol. I will sit you on the glass of my favorite pinball machine and try to make your bells and whistles go off."

It doesn't take me long to buckle myself in for the short ride to Last Resort. Once there, Zane takes me for a long ride on every surface in the bar. Thank goodness for soundproofing. We stay out of Bud's kitchen, but everything else is fair game.

Chapter Sixteen

The next week passes by in a flurry of activity. We visit Elaine on Tuesday and Thursday since Zane is leaving Friday morning. He seems a bit distracted with the planning of his trip. I thought they just saddled up and rode, but apparently there is a lot of logistical planning to get a group together.

I stay busy working on the tax software by day and waiting tables by night. Everywhere I look I'm reminded of our first official date. My favorite memory is of me sitting on the pinball machine as Zane made *all* of my bells and whistles ring.

It's Friday morning, and I am standing in the kitchen holding the baby and making coffee. I feel sad Zane is leaving for the weekend, but happy I can give him this time. I'm overjoyed he feels comfortable leaving me with his most precious possession.

"I don't want to leave you. Do you know how sexy you look standing in the kitchen in my T-shirt with baby drool dripping over your shoulder? I'm telling you; it does it for me."

"Shut up and leave us alone," I tease. "We have a whole day planned. We're having breakfast, then napping, lunch, and then a nap. Since Bud's brother is coming to help in the bar, I don't need to be downstairs until four."

"I'm a bit jealous of our boy. He gets you all to himself."

"Yes, and you get a break from both of us. Now get on your bike and ride before I change my mind. I'm going to miss you."

"I'm going. I'll call you tonight. I love you, and I'm going to miss you, too."

We spend several minutes kissing. It's like we're storing kisses for the days ahead.

"Be safe. Don't forget you're taking me on a date Monday night. It's my birthday, and I want you here safe and sound."

"I'll get home safely, sweets." He looks over his shoulder just before he closes the door.

Friday night, although crowded at the bar, goes smoothly. I spend the slower moments going upstairs to visit with Ashley and Aaron. I make sure she has plenty of junk food to keep her happy. Daisy stops by with her boyfriend, John, and we chat a bit and make plans to have lunch the following week.

Saturday doesn't go as smoothly as I would have liked. Tabitha shows up around six with a group of bikers. In all honesty, I had hoped that she would drop off the face of the earth. She sits with her group, but follows me with her eyes wherever I move. She approaches me as I pour a draft beer.

Her words are slurred, and it is obvious she isn't in the right frame of mind. She folds herself over the bar and tells me I have stolen her boy. I am certain she is referring to Aaron until she says that she fucked him first.

It doesn't take long for Bud and his brother to escort her out and send her on her way. I worry about her driving drunk. I also worry about the people driving on the same road. Bud settles my fears when he explains she is riding bitch. I've never liked that phrase until today, when I realize how fitting it is for her.

The last person exits the bar and the door is bolted closed. I bring the till upstairs and count it out like Zane has taught me. I put everything in the safe, pay Ashley, and ready myself for bed.

I lie down for the night knowing Aaron will be up in a few hours. Tucked into the much-too-large bed, I doze off to sleep thinking about Zane.

Something wakes me. It's that feeling something is wrong. I listen intently to see if I can hear anything in the house, but I hear nothing. Climbing out of bed as quietly as possible, I tiptoe down the hallway to check on the baby. I gaze into the crib and find him fast asleep. I shake my head at my overactive imagination. My first thought was Tabitha had broken in to steal the baby back.

I cover him and begin to walk down the hallway when I hear someone in the living room. I hear the unmistakable sound of someone tripping over Aaron's play matt. I do it myself every day, so I have that sound memorized.

I run to Aaron's room. Turn off the nightlight and pick up the first object I can find. I have no idea what's in my hand, but it seems hard enough to bludgeon someone with it. I will fight that bitch, or die trying.

The sounds of footsteps get louder as they get closer. I watch as the door opens slowly. I'm the only thing that stands in between Aaron and the intruder, and there is no way they're going to get their hands on my baby.

"Stop where you are," I call out. "If you come any closer I'll be forced to shoot you." I'm hoping I sound convincing.

The light blinds me as the intruder flips the switch. I

let out a guttural cry as I lunge at my attacker and hit him with the object in my hand. A loud crash echoes throughout the room. I am like a woman possessed—hitting, scratching and biting anything I can reach.

"Alexa, it's me. Stop!" I adjust to the light and see it's Zane. I've attacked him with a blue piggy bank that shattered at his feet.

"Damnit, Zane, you scared the shit out of me. What are you doing home?" I look him over and see that I've drawn blood on his arms in various places. He seems to be babying his left hand, which is dripping blood. "Oh my God, I hurt you. Let me see that." I pull his hand toward me and see a decent-sized gash on the fleshy part of his palm.

"I'm okay. Check on the baby and meet me in the kitchen." He shakes his head at me and chuckles all the way down the hall.

I turn around to look at Aaron, who has slept through the entire event.

"Let me see you. I'm so sorry." I hold his hand under the water to make sure his wound gets flushed out. "Tabitha came into the bar today and she was mad and drunk. I thought she had broken in and wanted to take our baby."

"Sweetheart, she wants nothing to do with *our* baby.

She's interested in herself only. I went to our room first, and when you weren't there, I figured you were with him. I didn't want to scare you, so I tried to be quiet in case you had fallen asleep rocking him. As soon as I opened the door, you attacked."

"I'm sorry; I was protecting the baby." I bandage his cut, which isn't too bad, and put antibiotic ointment on his bite marks.

"You were like an angry lioness protecting her cub." He pulls me into his arms.

"I wouldn't let anyone hurt him." Biting nervously on my lower lip. I ask, "Why are you home? If I had known, I wouldn't have attacked you."

"I missed you. I took care of what I needed to, and I realized that being with you and Aaron is so much more fulfilling than a bike ride."

"You arrive at your own house and get the crap beaten out of you. I'm so sorry." I bury my face in his chest, so embarrassed by my behavior.

"Do you have any idea how sexy that was? You're a force to be reckoned with. I don't feel like the victim here. The only victim is what used to be a blue ceramic pig. Remind me never to buy you a gun, you would shoot first and ask questions later." My heart drops into the pit of my stomach realizing how true that statement is. I could have really hurt him.

"I'm so sorry, but you shouldn't sneak up on people. For a large man, you're nearly silent." I back away from him and give him another once over. He has a few bruises and cuts, but all in all, he looks pretty good for a man who was just attacked.

"I'm sorry you had to deal with Tabitha. She'll continue to be a problem until she hooks up with someone else. That's my fault, and I apologize."

"She took off on the backseat of another man's bike, so she may be out of our hair for a while. I can't blame her, now that I've had you, I want to keep you."

"Shit, Alexa, you fight hard to keep what's yours. The only reason I'm probably not out cold is because I saw a shadow coming at my head, and I raised my hand as a reflex." He mimics the movement, and I can see I would have hit him smack on the side of the face if he hadn't deflected with his hand.

"Is there anything I can do for you?" I lay my head on his sternum and wait for his answer.

He simply says, "Let's go to bed."

In the short amount of time it takes us to get to the bedroom, he comes up with all sorts of ideas that would make him feel better. We spend the rest of the night in bed. I try hard to heal his wounds through love therapy, and he sets out to reward me for my bravery. It's quite a nice salve for both of us.

Sunday arrives, and we both lie exhausted waiting for Aaron to wake up. After last night's commotion, he awakened around five in the morning and went back to sleep as if nothing had transpired at the foot of his bed. While I fed him, his dad cleaned up the remains of the blue pig and laid him to rest in the trash.

With our coffee in our hands, Zane insists on watching the headline news. He scrolls through the channels as if he's looking for something in particular. I'm too tired to care. He stops on a national new station and asks me to look up.

The area is familiar and then I realize that the news crew is standing in front of my old house.

"Holy shit, Zane. What the hell is happening?" His face shows zero emotion. My heart begins to beat rapidly. I zone in on the picture and pray to myself Zane didn't make good on his threat to kill Tyler. It's not that I don't want him to pay for his wrongdoings, but I don't want Zane caught up in it.

The camera pans out to the crowd; hundreds of bikers

with the BFK logo on their jackets hold signs that say Tyler
Hasen is an abuser of women and very small children. The
news reporter goes on to explain the mission of Biker's for
Kids and says that she has never seen them come out in
such large numbers. This is obviously a very evil man.

In the distance, you can see someone pull the curtains
back slightly and then promptly let them fall.

"Please don't be mad at me. Like you, I protect
what's mine. Tyler had a bit of karma coming back to him.
This is part of my birthday gift to you. The other half I'm
hoping will arrive tomorrow."

"I'm not mad at you. I'm shocked that you pulled this
off in such a short period of time. How many bikers are
there?"

"There are only about five hundred right now, but
there are over ten thousand across the United States. They
don't mess around with men who abuse woman or children,
and Tyler did both. His house will be covered for weeks or
until he gives into our demands."

"What are your demands?" I turn around to look at
him.

"I don't want to spoil anything. Let's just wait and
see. Sometimes it takes a little longer for them to come
around." He turns off the television and pulls me into his

lap. We watch Aaron play on his play mat until Claire arrives.

The bar is fairly slow for a Sunday and Zane sees I'm fading fast. He sends me upstairs to climb into bed. Falling asleep has never felt this good.

I wake to the smell of something cooking. I can't believe I slept the entire night. Poor Zane must be exhausted. I slip out of bed and into the kitchen to rescue him.

On the counter is a waffle maker. The batter oozes slightly from the side. The coffee pot is full, and both of my boys are swaying to some secret music that's playing only in Zane's head. I creep up behind him and wrap my arms around his middle.

"Good morning, birthday girl. I hope you feel rested. You were sleeping like the dead when I came to bed."

"I was so tired. I hit the bed and was out. Let me take over, and you can rest for awhile."

"Not a chance, love. It's your birthday and as Abbamonte's, we would be remiss if we didn't pamper the woman who makes our lives wonderful. Have a seat. Aaron has whipped up some amazing waffles for breakfast, and I made the coffee."

He places Aaron in the bouncy chair by my feet, and

I spend the next few minutes making faces and crazy noises to get the smile I'm after. His little face lights up as I blow raspberries his way.

The boys go out of their way to pamper me the rest of the day. We enjoy a picnic in the park. We stop by Daisy's where Zane picks out and purchases a few more dresses for me. We stop by Walmart so he can fill the cart with Nutty Bars. On our way home, I notice cars in the bar parking lot.

"I invited Bud and his brother over for a BBQ." I can see he's holding something back; it's obvious that six cars aren't needed to deliver two men to the bar.

"Surprise!" the crowd calls out as we walk inside Last Resort. The volume is so loud, Aaron gets startled and begins to cry. It strikes me as funny he can sleep through yelling and the slaughter of his ceramic pig, but the shouting in the bar is his undoing.

I pull him into my arms and whisper softly into his ear. He calms immediately to the soothing sound of my voice. I wonder if all mothers feel like this. I feel like my boy knows that I'll keep him safe and secure. I will never let him down. I will never get to hold the baby I lost or soothe his or her cries. Having Aaron is like a healing balm though. Zane entrusting this treasure into my care is exactly what I have needed to feel valued.

I glance around the room. The bar is full of friends and neighbors. Zane makes me sit in the center of the room while everyone comes over to greet me. The first person walks slowly, but her smile tells her story. Elaine shuffles to my side where she takes a seat and the baby. Her baby sling is already in place. Bud breezes by to say hello and hands me a brand new ceramic pig. I look at Zane who just shrugs and looks away. Bud heads to the kitchen to make food for everyone.

Guests who approach me have some sort of a piggy bank in their hands. I know every single person from Trudy to Abrahm. They've become my family.

"What's with the banks, Zane?" I ask, even though I can make an educated guess. I know how it works in a small town. There are no secrets.

"I simply told everyone you had an angry obsession with ceramic banks. You're going to need a supply of ready ammunition." He laughs until he cries. I watch a tear slide down his cheek.

I look around me and realize a family isn't always who you're born to, but who you choose. And it seems not only have I chosen this family, but they have also chosen me.

The door to the bar opens, and I'm shocked to see

who arrives. My dad walks slowly forward and approaches Zane first. His sad eyes look to me, but he doesn't approach right away. My mother and sister come directly toward me.

"Oh, honey. I'm so sorry," she says. "We were so tied up in our own problems that we didn't take a minute to think about yours. We're terrible parents." A tear slips down her cheek.

I ponder my mom's statement for a minute. Yes, they are terrible parents, but what will it serve me to beat them with the facts. I stand up to give her a big hug, and I whisper in her ear. "When you know better, you do better."

I shift backward into a wall of muscle; his strong arms circle my waist as he turns me to face him. His lips hover near my ear.

"Your dad and Tyler have come to an amicable agreement; he will return half of what he stole from your dad. The house will be sold, and all proceeds will be donated to children in need. Although, only five hundred bikers were present, the club totals ten thousand bikers and they can make their presence known for quite a while. He's not as stupid as I thought. Happy Birthday, sweets."

"You're such a wonderful man, Zane Abbamonte. When I left Los Angeles, I thought my compass was broken, but it was working the whole time. It led me to my true north—to you. I love you."

"I love you, too." He kisses me gently before he backs up a bit. "Should we introduce your parents to their first grandchild? They're going to have to get used to him right away if we plan to give him a sibling soon."

"How soon?" I ask as I look into his eyes. They dance with mischief and mayhem, and nothing has ever looked so sweet.

Epilogue

"Can you grab the baby bag?" I ask as I rush out of our bedroom and into the kitchen.

"I got it," he says as he turns the corner. Aaron rests on his hip. As soon as he sees me he begins the sweetest mantra ever uttered.

"Ma ma ma ma ma."

"Yes, sweetie, I'm here." I gently pinch his cheek and rub his long brown curls. It's going to break my heart when they cut them off today, but his dad insists we start a tradition. "It's your birthday and you're getting your first haircut. Daddy thinks you look like a little girl. I think you look like a young warrior."

"Did you take your vitamin today?" Zane asks.

"Yes, it's hard not to when you deliver it to me in bed every morning." I think he feels the need to offset my Nutty Bar obsession with a daily vitamin infusion.

"I'm just protecting what's mine." He leans in and warms my insides with a kiss.

"We have to go. Everyone will be there, and we'll be late."

We pull up in front of the barbershop to find nearly half the town has shown up for little man's first cut. I watch as Zane sits in a chair with our baby on his lap. The barber makes a great fuss over Aaron before he moves in with his scissors. A few snips later and his baby face has morphed into a little boy.

I bend over and collect the curls from the floor. Tears stream from my eyes as I carefully place them in an envelope.

Zane kneels beside me and lifts my chin so that I'm looking into his eyes.

"It will grow back," he says, trying to comfort me.

"Oh, Zane, it's not the hair. It's just he's growing up so fast. He's already walking, and he's starting to talk. I'm not happy he's a huge fan of the word no, but I feel like things are moving so fast." I wipe the errant tears from my face and stand up.

I look over my shoulder and see everyone staring at me. My father is holding Aaron in his arms as my mother peppers Aaron with kisses. It's so nice to see they have turned out to be better grandparents than parents. Since my last birthday, they have visited every other weekend without fail. My dad has become the most attentive father ever. I often wonder if losing what you had makes you appreciate what you have.

"Let's head next door for his pizza party." Zane pulls me to his side and walks us into Luigi's. It's only fitting Aaron has his birthday party where his dad and I had our first date.

I look over at the corner table where we sat that night. I remember thinking it was the first day of the rest of my life, but now I know every day I spend with Zane is the best day of my life.

We enjoy an afternoon with family and friends. My eyes go in search of my two boys. I find Zane and Aaron walking toward me. The room becomes silent as they approach.

"Ma ma ma ma ma," Aaron chants as he toddles up to me. I reach down to pick him up.

In Aaron's hand is a blue velvet box.

"What do you have there?" I ask as he drops the box in my lap.

Zane kneels in front of me. His eyes glow with excitement as I slowly open the small box. He removes the ring and places it on my left hand.

"Please marry me?" he asks with love in his voice and passion in his eyes. "What do I have to do to get what I want?"

I rub my flat stomach and consider his question. "All you had to do was ask, Zane. Oh, and you can give Aaron a sister," I say and wink at him. I look up with hope in my eyes and love in my heart.

"Deal We'll name her Brie."

"Can't we wait to see her before we name her? You know how I am about names."

"You'll get lots of practice with names. By the time we get to the letter Z, we should have managed to get one of our kid's names right." He picks Aaron and me up from the chair together and swings us around. He never sees the stunned look on my face.

When I left L.A. and headed north, I wasn't expecting to find love. I was content to live my life alone. Call it fate, or providence, but whatever you call it, it delivered Zane to me. He saw me for the woman I am, an integral part of a family, a valuable member of a community, and now, the mother of a small boy. I arrived broken, stripped of dignity and hope, but love prevailed. Hope and joy have been rekindled. Tyler lost and I won—love won. My future looks bright because a man stopped for a stranger and gave her a chance. My future looks bright because a woman was picked up by a stranger, and gave her heart a chance on love.

An excerpt from

The Dean's List

Hunger gripped my stomach. Food had become a luxury item I couldn't afford. When I opened the cupboard this morning the shelves were bare except for the box of microwave popcorn and the remnants of Cornflakes strewn across the soiled contact paper.

I'm told that sex sells. Tell that to the cheap bastards who come to The Grind and gawk at the bikini baristas. While I froth their coffees and warm their cinnamon buns, they stare.

I dumped the jar that contained way more quarters than dollars on the table. The change clattered across the worn Formica and plopped onto the pleather bench of my favorite booth. It was here that I tallied my tip totals while the afternoon sunlight slanted in the window.

Today was a bear market day. Forty dollars would hardly pay my weekly transportation costs. How was I supposed to make my rent and eat?

Pride had kept me from asking for help, but I was

going to have to call Jade. From the little I'd seen of her lately, she appeared to be weathering the economic downslope better than I. She'd have a plan, she always did. I dropped my head to the table with a thunk, closed my eyes, and silently asked the universe for a solution.

"River, are you trying to knock yourself out?" Jade's appearance startled me. I'd been asking for a solution and here she was, standing in the center of the dead coffee shop with the smell of stale coffee and burned toast filling the air.

Without effort, she slid in beside me and dragged me into her thirty-eight double Ds. The way she stayed upright defied everything I'd learned in physics.

"Oh, Jade, I'm so glad you're here." Catlike eyes the color of moss peeked from behind the curtain of her raw, honey-colored hair. "I'm running out of options. I need a real job, and I need it now. I need one that pays a shitload of cash and lets me off when I have to study. Classes start next week. I need a miracle." Desperation accented every syllable. I wasn't one to exaggerate and Jade knew it. For me to say things were bad, they had to be beyond dismal.

"Girl, there aren't any miracles, only solutions. How bad is it?"

"This month I have to decide if I want to eat or ride the

bus. It's a conundrum because if I walk I get hungry, if I
ride the bus I get hungry. I'm just so tired of being hungry."
I hardly recognized my voice. The whine sounded more
like a sulky teen than the independent woman I was. "My
student loan is due. My phone is close to being silenced.
How in the hell do you survive?"

Jade leaned back, gaining distance. Her expression was
guarded. Her eyes skimmed my body. Today was career
day at The Grind, and I'd dressed up as a naughty nurse.
My stethoscope hung from my neck all the way to my bare
belly. My white bra was embellished with two red crosses,
one on each breast. My panties had a matching cross that
covered my crotch. We pushed the line when it came to city
code but a girl had to eat.

Jade eyed the girl behind the counter who was busy
studying her recent manicure. On the counter sat her empty
tip jar. "You look better than anyone who works here and
you're obviously making more money."

"This outfit used to make me bank, but with the stupid
stock market falling, gourmet coffee isn't a must-have for a
lot of brokers. I'm hoping tomorrow will be better. It's
pasty day." Maybe if I wore the tassels and gave demos on
how they spun, I could make enough to buy a used
textbook for my International Business class as well as a

bus pass. Big dreamer. At this point, I couldn't afford the lead in my mechanical pencil.

It hadn't always been this bad. I'd lost the Sunday shift from last semester, and with less tips, which had previously been an added bonus, my situation had become dire.

She gave me a warm, sisterly look—the kind that said, *I could take care of this.* And I was desperate enough to want to climb inside Jade's world and take shelter. *She had it together.* Somehow.

"What if I could help you get a job where you wore more clothes, most of the time, and made more money in a week than you do in a month?" Jade spoke in one long sentence, her pitch rising to the finish. When she reached the end, she held her breath and waited.

"I'd tell you to sign me up. It would have to be a step up from working here. The average customer at The Grind is middle-aged, white collar, and horny. Nice enough, but they don't come for the coffee." Yep, the brew was just a bonus.

Jade looked out the window seemingly absorbed by the rush of Wall Street traders racing back from lunch. She let out her breath, and then inhaled until I thought her lungs might burst. She was sucking in more than oxygen. Courage?

"Let's talk white collar and horny. What I'm about to tell you can't be repeated. I swear if it gets out, the FBI, CIA, and Homeland Security will come to arrest you. They'll fight over you and tear you from your top to your toes."

"If you're trying to scare me, you're failing. You don't have the fear factor. You wear Hello Kitty pajamas and drink caramel lattes for God's sake. Who could be afraid of someone who likes cats and caramel?"

"Don't underestimate the strength and power of a caramel macchiato. Show me a double and I'll show you fear. The caffeine alone is deadly."

From the deep recesses of her purse, she pulled out two energy drinks and handed me one. They were the kind of drink you bought for purpose rather than pleasure, and I wondered why I would need three hundred milligrams of caffeine after my shift had ended.

"Are you an assassin? Is that how you keep so damn fit?" I popped the top on the can of Bang and thought it ironic.

"No, I'm not killing anyone, but if you don't pay attention I might begin with you. Remember when I told you I was working in hospitality?" Her voice softened to a purr. "Well, that's the truth. I'm very hospitable." The words brushed past her lips like a lover's kiss.

"What the hell are you talking about? Aren't you the concierge at that fancy place on Fifth Avenue?" I swore she said she was the concierge. Maybe she'd said something about customer satisfaction. Hell, with the clothes she wore, she had to be raking in the tips.

"I never told you I was the concierge. I told you I was in charge of making sure clients' needs are met. I tried to get a job when I graduated, but you know a bachelor's degree doesn't cut it anymore. That's why you're here." She slipped from the booth and sat across from me. Something big was going down and she was distancing herself. "Have you ever heard of The Dean's List?"

The high-octane drink was beginning to thrum in my veins. "Um, yeah…I made the list in my sophomore, junior, and senior year. As a freshman, I was still figuring things out." What did that have to do with making moola?

Jade scooched and settled into the far corner of the booth. I moved myself so I sat directly in her line of sight.

"No, think about rumors. I'm talking about 'The Dean's List.'" She emphasized the word *Dean's*. "Think in terms of secret societies, like the Illuminati or the Freemasons."

"Are you trying to recruit me for a religious sect?

Count me out. Religion and I don't see eye to eye." Jade knew I was the poster child for what *not* to do as the daughter of a pastor. When I was caught blowing the mayor's son behind dad's pulpit, I was told I was going to hell. But, I gave that boy a boner-fied religious experience.

"Shut up and let me explain." Her black look silenced me. "The Dean's List is an exclusive group of people who meet to propel the university and its students toward success."

"Perfect, what can they do for me?" Her guarded look told me she intended to dance around the truth. In fact, I knew Jade well enough to know that she'd create an overpass to avoid it completely. "Get to the point." I didn't have time to dawdle. I needed to decide whether to ride the bus home or jump in front of it.

She tapped her fingers across the tabletop like she was typing an overdue thesis. "The Dean's List is about students seeking 'sponsorship' from members in their field of study. These members can be very 'accommodating.'" Her use of finger quotes around the word sponsorship and accommodating had me tilting my head.

"You're still speaking a different language. Plain English. Now. If I didn't know better, I'd think you were asking me to prostitute myself."

"Let me explain." Her shocked expression told me I'd hit a bulls eye.

My heart pitched forward, then tumbled swiftly into the hollow pit of my stomach. I kept my voice low. "Shit. You *are* asking me to become a hooker. There's no way you've been dishing yourself up for dollars. No. Fucking. Way." Prostitution wasn't a gig I could see Jade participating in. She was always so…so above board. I'd have been less shocked if she'd told me she were a man.

Her eyes shifted to every corner of the shop. Her body relaxed when we appeared to be alone. There was no one close enough to hear her secrets. Hell, The Grind would be like a morgue for the remainder of the day.

"Shhh, prostitution is such an ugly word." Her voice became uncharacteristically small. "I have a couple of advisors, also known as mentors or sponsors. They're successful members of their community. They work in hospitality management—my specialty. They donate obscene amounts of money to the university—my program. They take care of their own—me. And in exchange, I take care of them." She pulled the high throttle drink to her lips and drank like a marathon runner who'd just crossed the finish line.

"You screw men for money? How many men? Does

the school support this?" I leaned forward and mouthed the words. "Do you fuck them on the regular?" How did I miss her pimpin' her pussy for cash? We hadn't hung out as much over the last few months. I had missed her, but we were both busy with studies and our part-time jobs. Or so I'd thought. *This* is not what I'd expected.

She slapped the table and glared at me. I hadn't seen that look since the day we graduated from high school, when she told me we were moving to New York. "River. Listen." Her voice demanded compliance and I'd listen, because whenever Jade had a plan, my life inevitably got better. "I know this is sounding weird to you, but it's important this doesn't go anywhere. Got it?"

"It's a little late to get my sworn affidavit, don't you think? I never told your mom that you spent Fourth of July being a groupie for that grunge band. I never told Mr. Esly that your grandma didn't really die when you skipped finals week. You know me."

She reached over and held my hand just a little too firmly. Handholding could only mean some serious shit was going down.

"Okay, well... The Dean's List only takes graduate students. Educated men and women. No giddy juveniles. Like you, I was broke. An opportunity came along and I took it."

"You. This. How long?" I would consider myself the worst of friends if she told me years.

Jade made no excuses. It wasn't her way. "Several months." She released my hand and leaned back in the booth. With her fingers laced, she turned them inside out and pressed them forward.

Pop.

Pop.

Pop.

The disgusting sound of knuckles cracking made me cringe. My discomfort gave her the edge and she knew it. She had my full attention.

"Get on with it." She was going to try to sell me on the possibility of selling myself. *Had my life come to this?*

"Three positions are open and interviews are happening now, but there are only two positions you qualify for since you don't have a penis." Her tone was matter of fact.

"I have to interview to be a fucking prostitute?" My heart pounded so loudly I was certain Jade could hear it across the booth. *A prostitute? Really?*

She gave me a slow disbelieving headshake. "How many times have you had a one-night stand and received nothing but a hangover and a dirty snatch?" She lifted her perfectly plucked brows in question.

"You make it sound like I'm already a whore." I swear she flinched at my reply. "I'm not loose. I'm experimental." I tried to lessen the tension I was feeling with witty commentary. "Hell, the average woman has had six sexual partners by the time she's thirty. At twenty-five, I've had eight. So… I'm an overachiever."

"I never said you were a whore. I'm only telling you that you can earn a lot of money being an overachiever." A sly smile lit up her features. "Your number, when divided, doesn't add up to one a year. That's so far below ho—we can't count it. You're treading on virgin territory and we can change that." Her eyes danced with delight.

"I don't get it, Jade. How did I not know?" I let my head fall forward in shame. I had no idea what my best friend had been up to.

"I had to keep the secret in order to participate. I had to participate in order to survive." Her strong voice had lost its power. "Right now, you're where I was several months ago."

"And you want me where you are now." Could I consider it? Could I afford not to? Elbows on the table, I laced my hands and rested my chin on the flat of my knuckles. The busy sounds of New York dimmed as my mind raced and raged and rallied. *Could I?* "I'm listening, tell me the rest."

"My boss asked me yesterday if I had any pretty friends who could fill the empty positions. I thought of you, but I wasn't sure. With your dad being a man of God, I didn't know if you'd risk his wrath. I know your relationship with them isn't perfect or pretty but…"

"'Isn't pretty' is like saying herpes is a form of chapped lips. Seeing them twice a year doesn't keep me connected or establish a relationship. Go on."

Jade was the star debater in high school. She could sell a purple cape to Superman. I was curious to see how she'd sell this.

"You'd be set up with people who have influence in your field. Being an MBA you have a broad reach, and with your looks you'll have a big audience. We're talking about lots of men with boatloads of money."

"Lots of men? Okay. Great. But are you forgetting this whole thing is illegal?" I looked at her with wild-eyed shock.

"It's not illegal. Who doesn't barter for goods and services? It's muddy at best. You might barter for clothes, jewelry, vacations, cars, and of course there is also cash.

They're gifts, and the mentors can be very generous. We're talking Prada and Gucci, Channel and Dior. Sleeping with a date is not illegal."

Gifts of that magnitude weren't given to girls like me. I was thrift store and Goodwill—the hand-me-down princess.

"Why would a man pay that much for one night?"

"We give them something they can't get anywhere else. It's like going to the on-campus shop and buying a monogrammed sweatshirt. You know what you're getting when you shop there. It's high quality, not cheap, and it behaves the way you expect it to. Think of yourself as a luxury purchase."

"I'm not a sweatshirt, Jade. One size doesn't fit all." Of all the things to compare me to, couldn't she have come up with something more alluring than a sweatshirt?

"That's where you're wrong. You're adaptable. You can fit in anywhere." Jade pulled her ringing phone from her purse, looked at the screen, ignored the call, and tossed it back into her purse. "Don't let your parents destroy your self-respect."

My parents? They annihilated my self-esteem long ago.

"I am intrigued. What do I have to do?"

"You get to eat at Michelin Star restaurants, stay in

five star hotels, and come all the time. Who wouldn't love that?"

So the mentors were good lovers. Her argument had merit. But could it be that simple? Could I do casual sex for cash?

"How many men do I have to entertain?" What else would I call it? Escort? Date? Fuck? It all came down to money for sex.

"You can do as many, or as few as you wish. I started out with several and then worked my way to two. I'm engaged in 'school activities' four nights a week. On occasion my mentors have me travel with them."

"Oh my God, so when you said the school was sending you to that conference in California, you were with your mentors?" She was gone for a week and came back with a sun-kissed glow and a new wardrobe. Shortly after that trip she moved into a new apartment. One I'd yet to see. "The apartment you're in… is it… Oh, you little lying slut. You told me you had to move closer to work. You moved *into* work." She's my best friend. How had she so easily been lying to me about all of this?

"I struggled to keep things under wraps when you and I lived together. They wanted more time, and I couldn't give more without you getting suspicious." Her hands darted all over the place while she talked about her situation. "I was given an ultimatum. I had to give them more time or give them up. We bartered, and I ended up with the best possible outcome." It was funny to watch her get riled. She was usually so unflappable.

"You could have told me." I felt… betrayed. *I didn't think we had any secrets from each other.*

"I couldn't. That was against the rules." Her voice was tinged with sadness and regret.

"Wow, okay. So, what happens to the apartment if they dump you?" I didn't want to bring up the possibility, but it was something to consider. She'd only been in her new place for a few months. A few months and I'd been clueless.

"My mentors signed a year contract with me regardless of whether they use the service or not. They don't live with me. They visit four nights a week. Sometimes it's more, sometimes it's less. I'm good for a year."

"I don't know what to say." There was too much information to process. Jade. A prostitute. Wow. She looked happy. Was *I* happy for her? Hell, I think I was.

"You don't have to say anything. I know what you're going through." She looked around the coffee shop. "Dead-end job, no prospects, and dreams bigger than you can afford." We had both been struggling, but then things had changed for her. Only moments before, I'd wanted to climb into her world. Well, perhaps I could.

"Tell me about these mentors. Are they old and decrepit?" The word *mentor* brought all kinds of images to mind. Dirty old men shaking with Parkinson's and leering at my naked body topped the list. I looked around the café and realized that exact scenario happened here all the time, and I rarely got more than a fiver. I certainly never got an apartment.

"No, one of my mentors is forty-five. The other is fifty-two. I'm not saying the mentors can't be old. I've seen men as old as eighty and as young as thirty-five. On average, they're between forty and sixty."

I've always liked older men. Not grandpa old, but ten to twenty years older is perfect for me. I'm attracted to the confidence found in mature men.

"Sixty. Fuck." My nervous laughter drew the attention of several patrons who had recently arrived.

She leaned in toward me and whispered, "Early on, my bits hardly saw action. Many of them only want to come on your face or between your tits." She raised her brows and gave me a coy look that probably melted the resolve of every man she'd ever been with.

"You're shitting me. You made money letting men—" How could I chide her, I'd done worse for less.

"Shhh. That's part of the negotiation. You fill out a form very much like an employment application. It has several sections on limits. If you hate anal, then you check the *no* box. If you don't like sex toys or fucking in a Jell-O bath, then you can write that in. Generally speaking, the more open you are to trying things, the more popular you'll be."

"Jell-O baths? Really?" Nothing that a little soap and water couldn't remove I suppose.

"It could happen. Some of them just want to go to dinner and talk."

"They paid you to talk?"

"Yes."

"Unbelievable. I would want the talkers." Would it possible to get only the talkers?

"It's not that simple. After a couple of months of trying out several mentors, I was asked for exclusivity from one of mine. Basically, I see only him and his partner." She gave me a look that I recognized as her *don't judge me* look. "Yes, I do both of them. It works out well for all of us." Who was this woman and what had she done with my best friend?

"Partners? As in plural? Who are these men? I've never heard you mention anyone's name." These secrets had robbed me of my friend.

"That's part of the deal. They remain anonymous, and I get through my grad program debt free, well fed, and housed. It's my goal to build good relationships with these people. They're in my industry and they have the connections I need to succeed."

"Do you ever get attached to them? Aren't you afraid of falling in love?" Would it be possible to be in an intimate relationship and keep it superficial? Doesn't intimacy lead to love?

"Don't fall in love. I went into this knowing it wasn't a real relationship. It's a job. I give them what they want. They give me what I need. The only way to survive is to keep that in the forefront of your mind." Her tone seemed to fade as the words slipped hesitantly from her mouth.

"Are they married?" *How would I feel about being the other woman?* I may have had sex with more than a few men, but I'd never cheated on anyone, and I was never the girl that anyone cheated with.

"The men I see are single as far as their profile states. I know it's a lot to absorb, but the call I got was from my boss. She wants me to bring you to her office for an interview and to size you up if you're interested. What do you think?"

What do I think? How does one get sized up for a job peddling sex?

I turned in the booth and looked around the mostly empty coffee shop, spotting my co-worker. She rolled her eyes at some possibly cheesy comment the man in front of her at the counter said. No more shitty comments and equally shitty tips. *What did I have to lose?*

"Let's go. Can I at least go home and change? I'm not sure wearing my nursing uniform is appropriate." I looked down and considered my voluptuousness. Despite the placement of the red crosses, these suckers had only made me forty today.

Was I *really* considering this? This wasn't how I was raised, but given my parents' opinion of me, it wouldn't have been too far outside their expectations.

About the Author

Kelly Collins writes with the intention of keeping the love alive.

Always a romantic, she is inspired by real time events mixed with a dose of fiction. She encourages her readers to reach the happily ever after and bask in the afterglow of the perfectly imperfect love.

Kelly lives in Colorado with her husband of twenty-five years. She loves hockey and stops for shiny objects.

Other Books by

Kelly Collins

Set Free

Set Aside

The Dean's List

Honor Roll

True North

Cole For Christmas

Tempo

The Decadent Series

Just Dessert

Brownie Points

Whipped

Blue Ribbon Summer

Meet Me Romance Novellas

Meet Me Under the Full Moon (Book 1)

Meet Me On the Dance Floor (Book 2)
Meet Me In the Middle (Book 3)
Meet Me In Secret (Book 4)

Made in the USA
San Bernardino, CA
02 August 2016